Stand Tall

By Richard Vollmer

Table of Contents

Prologue

It is late in the second war between Earth and Novus. Earth is losing, and they know it.

Thirty years earlier in the final deal that ended the First Interstellar War, Earth was made to cede control over the world of Dominion, its largest and most promising colony. It was not long after Dominion gained independence that its central government collapsed. In the years following, numerous territories and fiefdoms were formed, each pursuing their own goals. Rampant infighting ensued, and in turn almost total economic collapse. Furthermore, the Earth Union had initiated a policy of isolating Dominion whenever possible. This was first done with blockades, which were quickly disbanded when Novus intervened. An unofficial policy of hiring privateers to patrol the surrounding space then followed. Despite anti-piracy efforts from the newly formed United Trade Coalition, commerce between Dominion and other worlds soon ceased. The world fell into technological decline, leaving it weak. Now, Earth is looking to perform a land grab so that something may be gained despite the impending defeat.

Dominion is ripe for conquest.

Chapter 1 – Antonin

Hecate Space Station, Earth

As quickly as he could, Antonin Bykov stuffed his company apparel down the garbage disposal. First, the khaki pants, then the black collared shirts with the bronze company logo on the breast. Next went some of the various knick-knacks around his apartment. A gold keychain, business cards, an employee of the month award. All of it rattled its way down the disposal the same. Next, he pulled out his handgun. It was company issued, and the serial number could be traced. He stared at it for a moment. He might need it. That'd be the last to go.

He tucked the pistol into his waistband and turned toward his dresser. Throwing open the drawers, he grabbed what clothes he had left, tossing them into a pile on the bed next to his duffel bag. Within moments the dresser was empty, and he turned towards the pile on the bed. Without the company wear, it was scant. "Yebat'!" He cursed under his breath as he began stuffing what was left of his clothes into the bag. Completely abandoning his usual sense of order, he had the bag packed and zipped up within seconds.

Hearing footsteps outside his door, he froze. Soon enough, the steps passed, and he exhaled heavily. He wiped the sweat from his brow. Best that he clean himself up real quick. He didn't need to give the guards at the terminal a reason to stop him. Stepping into the small bathroom

6

opposite his apartment door, he splashed his face with water from the sink and tried to neaten his hair.

"Idiots! We had a nice thing going! Why did they have to get involved in politics?" he muttered to himself. He stared at his reflection in the mirror. "It doesn't matter now." He grabbed a towel and dried himself. Just as he was finishing up, he heard a bang on the door.

Chapter 2 – Orientation

Six Months Earlier – Western Territories, Dominion

Up ahead, a few shots rang out, and the line moved forward a step. Keith winced at the sound. Gunshot after gunshot, combined with the bright Dominion sun, was not helping the headache. That, and he wasn't enjoying the burns on his ankles. Not that he could recall where they were from. Up ahead, a man with a red cross on his armband worked his way down the line.

"Look at me."

Keith looked up at the man, trying to stand straighter.

"Your legs work? Any ailments?" he asked.

"Legs work, and what?"

"Are you sick?"

"Just hungover, sir."

The man nodded. "Follow my finger. Both your eyes work?"

"Yeah." Keith squinted in the bright sunlight.

8

"Good. Open your mouth."

As Keith did this, the man grabbed him by the side of the head with a gloved hand and tilted his head back. He then nodded.

"Continue forward." He let go of Keith and moved on to the next guy.

Keith shook himself then looked up at the pale-yellow sky, trying to wish away the urge to throw up. Until yesterday his primary job was keeping razor cats away from Echo Ranch's cattle and tending to the crops. It was a good job, and probably one he should've stuck with. Instead, he'd signed up for this foolish endeavor. Another two shots rang out up ahead, and he'd reached the front of the line. Here, there was a table with a soldier sitting behind it, preparing a stack of papers and pens. The soldier looked up at Keith and pushed a sheet towards him.

"Sign."

Keith picked up the document and spent a moment looking over the letters of each word, unsure as to where to begin. A moment later, he spoke up. "I don't know how to read."

The soldier sighed and reached forward, pointing at two lines along the bottom. "Put your mark here, please."

Keith nodded and signed the paper. Kind of a 'K' with a circle around it, his personal signature.

The soldier took the document back and stared at it for a moment. "Close enough. Your name?"

"Keith Lane."

He filled something in at the bottom of the sheet before shoving it into a pile to his left. He then pointed over his shoulder. "Walk up to the line."

Another soldier stood at the line. Fifty meters away was a metal plate hanging on a stand, pock-marked with numerous bullet strikes.

"Shoot the target." This soldier went to hand Keith a rifle, but he declined.

"I've got my own already."

"Suit yourself." He leaned the rifle back up against an ammunition crate.

Keith brought his rifle up to his shoulder, an old lever-action he had inherited from his father. A moment later, he fired, and the target rang.

"Good shot, recruit. Can you do it again?"

"Yessir." He brought the rifle up again and took another shot, wincing at the ringing in his ears. None the less he hit the target, and the soldier checked something off on his clipboard.

"Join that group over there." The soldier pointed to a group of men to Keith's right.

Keith nodded and began the walk in that direction, rubbing his forehead. His headache was getting worse. Upon arriving at the next station, he was promptly handed a dark green armored vest and given instructions on how to put it on, along with the statement, "This vest and all its components are on loan to you. Do not trade with other personnel. Do not take the vest apart."

Yesterday, he'd joined the roving convoy of the "Unified Dominion Armed Forces." They had been broadcasting their message over the radio for the past few months, touting higher pay than the ranches were offering and an opportunity to unite Dominion. Keith thought the whole thing was silly, at least until he saw the convoy. It'd passed through in the morning, a line of trucks and armored vehicles packed to the brim with troops, singing songs and beckoning passersby to hop on board. Ultimately, Keith did jump on to one of the trucks and promptly spent the rest of the day – and night – drinking. It was a dumb thing to do, but who'd turn down a free beer? Or ten for that matter.

Unlike what the soldiers in the trucks wore, his vest looked worse for wear, being severely faded and tattered around the edges. As he strapped it on, he was met with a dank odor resonating from it. Overall, the prospects of this new job were looking less glamorous by the minute. After being issued their vests, they were given breakfast and something to drink, both of which were desperately needed. As soon as they'd finished, another soldier approached, beckoning them to stand up.

"Alright, gentlemen." He eyed one particularly hungover recruit still lying on the ground and tapped him with his boot. "I'm going to teach you all how to walk. Line up!"

At this, Keith did what he could to stand up straight, not that the soldier seemed that concerned with his posture. Within a few minutes, they'd formed into a rough block and were made to march around the field. As they made their rounds, the soldier would periodically stop to describe patches of ground. "This is where the mess tent will be set up. Your meals will be served here." "This is where the command tents will be set up. You are not to enter this area." At the end of the walk, they'd reached a line of small, one-man tents organized into blocks. Here, they were issued their own and taught how to set them up. Each was a simple thing, composed of a brown, oiled canvas and just long enough to lie in. Meanwhile, another group of recruits that'd already been through the process began setting up the camp.

Around mid-afternoon, they were given lunch. Keith finished his quickly, otherwise refusing to move.

He'd finally found a solid patch of shade and was intent on keeping it. His attention was then drawn to another recruit approaching him. Grunting, the recruit sat down cross-legged a few feet away. He was larger, and his vest was squeezed tightly around his gut.

"Hey kid, how you doing?"

Keith looked over and nodded. "Doing just fine."

"Man, you were funny last night."

Keith stared at him for a moment. He didn't recognize him. Apparently, "blacking out" from alcohol consumption was a real thing.

The man continued, "When you were dancing around the fire, man, I'm gonna have to steal some of your moves."

Keith nodded again. "I must apologize, I don't know your name."

"Name's Gazmend from the Belcher Ranch. You?"

"Keith, I'm a farmer. Echo Ranch." He reached forward and shook Gazmend's hand.

"Keith's got the moves!"

"Yeah, I guess so." He couldn't help but feel elated.

"Why'd they give you guys green armor?"

Keith looked over Gazmend's vest. Unlike his, it had black shoulder pads. "They sent me to right group. We all got these."

"How'd you do with the shooting?"

"Hit the target both times!"

"Not bad!" Gaz then stood up, turning to leave as quickly as he had arrived. "Was nice meeting you. I'll see you around."

"Sure thing!"

The next morning Keith and other new arrivals got into line, standing as straight as they could. This time, the soldiers berated them on their lack of posture and continued to do so until they resembled a line of planks. When the soldiers were finally satisfied, a particularly tall one approached their formation. Like the rest, he was fully armored from head to toe, his helmet concealing his face.

"Good morning, gentlemen," he started, beginning to pace. "I am Captain Kowal. Welcome to the Unified Dominion Armed Forces. Your service will lead us towards a better future, both for you, and all peoples." He then gestured towards a soldier to his left. "From now on, you will address these gentlemen as 'advisors.' They are here to help you, train you and will work to provide you with what you need for your time with us. We will refer to you as 'recruits.' Simple enough, yes?"

Everyone nodded.

"A few questions have come up about pay. Rest assured, you will be paid, and in the manner you so choose. For right now, I think a little orientation is in order." He stopped pacing and looked over the recruits in front of him. "Tell me, why are we here?"

Keith and those around him stood silently, not sure how to respond.

"A bunch of mutes. Beat your faces!"

Another advisor then stepped forward and shouted, "Pushups, now!"

Twenty pushups later, the recruits were standing again, mild perspiration on their brows. Kowal then asked again, "Why are we here?"

"To unite Dominion and defeat those that would hurt her," mumbled Keith, echoing the radio broadcasts.

"You!" The Kowal pointed at Keith. "Say that again!"

"To unite Dominion and defeat those that would hurt her!" repeated Keith, this time louder.

"Good!" He returned his gaze to the rest of the recruits. "We are here for you! We do not care where you came from. We care only that you are with us now. We will bring the peoples of Dominion together for a better future! A brighter future! Does that make sense, gentlemen?"

The recruits nodded. Kowal glared at them through his goggles. "Answer me out loud, recruits!"

"Yes sir!" Keith and the rest of the formation shouted.

He nodded. "We'll make an army of you yet." He then gestured towards an advisor next to him. "Mr. Thomas will be taking care of you from here on out. He is your new advisor, and you will do what he says. Good luck."

Without pause, Thomas stepped up and barked, "Hop to it, recruits! Move!"

The rest of the day was spent running or marching, depending on Thomas's mood. The rest of the week followed the same pattern: wake up, get shouted at, get into line. A few men tried to leave but were promptly caught, beaten, and made to run laps around the fields. As the advisors repeatedly said: They had signed the papers, now they were in it for the long haul.

Chapter 3 – Boot

Keith settled in with his lunch tray, trying to avoid contact with the chafe beneath his arms. The mess tent wasn't nearly large enough for all the recruits, so meals were done in short shifts, with recruits finding themselves pushed out as quickly as they stepped in. Today, Keith was lucky. He was among those on the last shift, so they didn't have to worry about getting kicked out by the next group, granting them a few extra minutes to enjoy the shade. Gaz then sat down across from him, unclipping the sides of his vest and letting the accumulated heat out.

"Oh, hey! How have you been?" asked Keith. He hadn't seen Gaz since they'd been separated into different groups.

Gaz looked up. "Keith, right?"

Keith nodded.

"Mhm." Gaz began eating from his tray. "What have you green-shoulders been up to?"

"Getting shouted at mostly. I should've paid better attention to the weapons briefings."

"Training with rifles?"

"Yeah."

Gaz nodded. "Not much of that on this end."

Keith looked at him questioningly.

"Running exercises," elaborated Gaz. "Not that I can shoot for shit anyway, but fucking aye." He exhaled and stretched out his legs. "I don't think I was made for running either."

Keith looked him over. He really wasn't. "What'd you do at Belcher Ranch? You one of the brewers?"

"Fermenting beer was never my thing. You?"

"Kept razorcats away from cattle. Occasionally fought with Gilleppo Ranch."

Gaz razed an eyebrow. "How'd that turn out?"

"Lots of yelling. I wasn't there the time one of our guys got shot."

"You're lucky."

"I guess so."

Before anything else could be said, a whistle could be heard. It was the advisors' way of saying lunch was over. At this, Keith stuffed his face with what was left on his tray and nodded at Gaz. "I'll see you around."

"Sure."

Keith then dropped off his tray at the wash station and ran to join his group. He'd been assigned to Group 17, a ten-man squad of green shoulders. From the onset, they'd been set to practicing with their issued rifles. These were crudely built things, many of which were missing parts and all of which rattled. At the very least, they worked, something which couldn't be said of the few weapons that Keith's Echo Ranch had at its disposal. That, and UDAF had ammunition for them. Never in his life had Keith practiced so much with a single weapon without fear of running out of cartridges for it.

However, despite this perk, he quickly came to question the UDAF's obsession with putting men into lines. The time spent on the range was short compared to the amount spent running or marching, and no matter what they were doing, it had to be done in a line. Skirmish lines, inspection lines, advancing lines. It didn't make sense. In the border conflicts between ranches, there was no need for such organization. If you could get the jump on the other side, you were good, and marching in a line never accomplished that.

The next week, Keith was surprised to see Gaz again as he and his group filed into the mess tent. Once he'd made it through the lunch line, he moved to the other side of the tent and sat down opposite him. He looked tired.

"Hey Keith, how you doing?" he asked.

"This chafing is killing me."

Gaz looked over Keith momentarily, eyeing the red patches along the sides of his rib cage.

"I know it's hot, but you really should wear a shirt under that."

Keith thought about it. "Yeah, you're right." After a few moments, he spoke up again. "I have a question."

"Sup?"

"What are we actually going to do?"

"I was listening in on some of the advisors. Some say that Earthers are coming."

Keith looked at Gaz, surprised. "I've heard about them, never seen one, though." Keith paused for a moment. "Well, maybe I have, my daddy was Earth-born."

"Mine too." Gaz paused. "Most of our fathers were, for that matter, though they may deny it. Earth abandoned us, probably before you were born. How old are you?"

"About to turn 18."

"Yeah, they left years before you were around. No one at your ranch taught you about this?"

"Never taught me to read either, straight to the fields. Nice of them to keep me around, though. Also got to keep my daddy's place."

"Mhm." Gaz looked at Keith for a minute, a hard expression on his face.

20

"It's not been bad, really," mumbled Keith, not sure how to continue.

"Yeah." Gaz didn't sound convinced. "Just make sure you're not getting taken advantage of."

"Can do." Keith then returned his focus to his food, finishing up before looking back up at Gaz. "The Earthers, do they have a problem with us?"

"Honestly, I don't know. I don't trust 'em." Gaz then leaned in a little closer, lowering his voice to a whisper. "I'd be careful around UDAF too. They're not from here."

"You talking across the ocean?"

"Possible."

"But how do you know?" Keith was starting to get an uneasy feeling in his stomach.

"Their stuff is too new." Gaz pointed over his should at a nearby truck. "I don't think those came from New Mantua." Seeing the expression on Keith's face, he spoke up again. "Sorry, I don't mean to freak you out, kid. I'm sure everything is going to be alright. I just joined up to see what this is all about."

"Alright." Within a few seconds, Keith's mind was already on to other things. "The advisors, I noticed they don't sweat? Well, at least not as much as us, and they wear more armor too!"

For a moment, Gaz had a somewhat amused expression on his face, then proceeded to explain. "They've got suits under that armor that keeps them cool. I'm sure if you ask one of them, they'll probably show you. Just do it during one of the breaks."

"Got it."

During the next break, Keith was looking around at the advisors, trying to find one that appeared somewhat approachable. They tended to stay in groups and stared down anyone that got near them. After a few minutes of searching, he found one, off at the edge of the field leaning against a tree, head down. With all the confidence he could muster, Keith walked straight up to the advisor, stopping about ten feet away.

"Excuse me, Advisor, sir." Despite previous briefings, Keith still wasn't sure how to properly address these men.

The advisor looked up at Keith and stood straighter. He was in full kit, every part of his body covered in armor plating with his helmet concealing his face. The only identifiable marking on him was an olive drab name tag on his chest that read "Amor."

"How can I help you?" he asked.

22

The advisor was nearly a head taller than Keith and wider. Keith looked up at him, noticing his own reflection in the advisor's goggles.

"I heard that you guys have suits that keep you cool."

"Yes."

There was an awkward pause.

"May I see it?" asked Keith.

"What's your name?" asked the advisor.

"Name's Keith. I'm a farmer."

"Sure, Keith." The advisor proceeded to undo his left gauntlet, eventually pulling it off before rolling up the sleeve of his battle dress. The layer underneath was a glossy plastic with subtle ribbing along the outside of the forearm and a vein-like pattern on the inside, all black and green in color. Keith stared at it, confused by the material. It looked like it was melded to the man's arm.

"Thank you," said Keith, perplexed and without much else to say.

"No problem." At that, the advisor pulled his sleeve back down and put his gauntlet back on.

Not sure how to proceed, Keith turned around and walked back to the camp.

Chapter 4 - Mount Up

This morning everyone was awoken earlier than usual, with the advisors shouting at the recruits to get their full kit together. Within a few minutes, they had gotten into line in the staging area, a task that they had become readily proficient in. Soon enough, Captain Kowal appeared, flanked by group leaders. Behind them, an unarmored man followed, a clipboard in hand. As the advisors approached their respective groups, the new man remained next to Kowal, jotting something down. Keith eyed him for a moment. Like the advisors, he wore an olive drab coverall and combat boots. Unlike the advisors, he lacked a helmet, exposing his incredibly pale skin and blonde hair. Squinting in the bright sun, the new man pulled down his large, mirror-sunglasses.

"Straighten up!"

Keith jumped as an advisor elbowed him. He then corrected his posture and faced forward. Once the advisors had finished inspecting the line, Kowal spoke.

"Good morning, recruits. Remind me, why are we here?" He looked at Keith.

"To unite Dominion and defeat those that would hurt her!" shouted Keith.

This time the advisor behind Keith slapped him on the shoulder, saying, "Atta-boy!" before continuing down the line. In the corner of his vision, Keith swore he could see the advisor flipping off the "new man."

"Excellent." Kowal took a deep breath. "Gentlemen, this is the day we've been preparing for: Earth is coming."

There was some grumbling among the older recruits, mostly Gaz's age or older. The younger ones like Keith were wide-eyed at the prospect.

"The oldest among you have seen this before. Earth only takes. They are here for your money, your land, your crops, even your children. Thirty years ago, you drove them off-world. Now they are back."

The grumbling intensified, even among the younger crowd.

"We will push them back, we will drive them off-world, and we will unite Dominion under one banner!" Kowal took a deep breath. "Gather your weapons. We'll be moving out shortly."

As opposed to the usual "dismissed," the advisors instead began shouting, ordering the recruits to pick up the pace and driving them into a fervor.

Keith ran to the entrance of his tent, grabbing his lever action and a leather bandolier packed with cartridges for it. Opening the action partially, he confirmed that it was loaded. He didn't know when exactly they'd be fighting, but he'd be ready. A nervous feeling then hit the pit of his stomach. He'd be fighting the giants soon, the men from Earth. It then occurred to him, had Earth done anything yet? He shook himself. No, it was just like a border conflict. Earth was on the wrong side, and he would push them out, just like when he worked for the foreman. He jumped as Gaz put a hand on his shoulder.

"Farmboy, you ready?"

"Hells yeah!" Keith said it more enthusiasm than he was feeling.

"Good, let's go."

They proceeded to the armory, which was already mobbed by recruits. Within a few minutes, a line of advisors had forced them back and were shouting at them to form up. Once Keith and Gaz made it through, they returned to the staging area at a jogging pace. At least a dozen large trucks had already positioned themselves at the northern edge of the field. Over the din, the advisors began shouting over a loudspeaker, "Black shoulders left, green shoulders right!" They repeated this phrase until the horde steadily began separating.

At this, Gaz grabbed Keith by the shoulder, looking him directly in the eyes. "Stay safe. I'll see you on the other side, alright?"

"You got it!" Keith had to shout to be heard over the rumble of engines and men.

As Gaz ran to join the rest of the black-shoulders, Keith turned back towards the trucks. Having found himself in the middle of the crowd, it was a solid ten minutes before he re-located his group and was ordered on board. When his time came, he climbed up into the back of a vehicle with nineteen other men. Almost immediately, the truck stuttered forward and joined the column. Looking around, Keith realized that nearly everyone on board were recruits, with only two advisors at the front of the bed. It wasn't like the column that had picked him up nearly two months before, fully kitted and ready to take on the world. Many of the men here still wore the clothes they arrived in.

Chapter 5 – First Contact

"Group 17! We will be providing fire support for the black shoulders. They will be the first to advance. You are not to move until we say so. You will not retreat unless we say so. Does this make sense?"

"Yes sir!" Keith and the other recruits answered simultaneously.

"Most importantly, do not fire your weapons until we say so. Anyone who does will be shot. Got it?" The advisor emphasized these last words.

"Yes sir." This time the response was more muted, some recruits angered by the threat but none willing to test it. Keith figured the advisor was exaggerating and didn't think much of it. He was more anxious for the wait to be over.

Keith then watched as another truck offloaded its passengers, only to be immediately met with advisors insisting that they quiet down. The process had repeated itself throughout the hot afternoon, with each successive group being led into the woods on either side. Further away, the murmur of more engines could be heard. Much to the chagrin of the recruits, it seemed that they would not be fighting today. Instead, they were ordered to sit among the trees quietly while the advisors gathered.

Looking around, Keith spotted the hunched figure of Gaz, sitting among his group of black shoulders. Hesitantly, Keith stood up and walked over.

"How you doin' Gaz?" asked Keith, kneeling next to him.

"I swear all this sitting is hurting me more than running would."

Keith couldn't help but smile. "What we got? At least a hundred here?"

"More than that." Gaz pointed back along the road. About a hundred meters down, more black shoulders and an advisor could be seen shuffling into the tree line.

Their conversation was then interrupted as an advisor approached, looking at Keith.

"Rejoin your group."

Keith looked up at him. "Yessir!"

The sun had since set below the trees, the sky turning from pale-yellow to bronze as darkness set in. The advisors handed out sealed ration packs, which quickly turned out to be a messy affair. Only a few recruits knew how to open them properly, and even fewer knew how to prepare them. At the same time, advisors handed out thin brown plastic sheets and ordered everyone to put them on.

After much grumbling, the recruits were made to comply. At one point, an older recruit attempted to explain the science behind thermal signatures, but his lecture fell on deaf ears. All the while, the advisors kept glancing up at the darkening sky. That night no one was permitted to turn on lights or start fires. Overhead, the roar of jet engines could be heard, their glow illuminating the treetops. At this, the men went silent. Earth was here.

When morning came, water bottles were handed out alongside word that they'd be fighting today. Once again, Keith checked both his rifles to make sure they were loaded. The time had finally come, and the worst thing he could imagine was his gun jamming at the wrong moment. Many of the others had taken to performing the same pre-battle rituals. The advisors just walked slow circles around the staging area like specters, whispering to each other via radio. When Keith finally got over the uneasy feeling in the pit of his stomach, the order went out to move.

Unlike training, there was no shouting. Instead, the advisors passed the word along quietly, and the men were made to move slowly through the thicket. Eventually, they came to the top of a hill overlooking a valley and were ordered to halt. Two large U-shaped craft could be seen at the bottom of the valley, one appearing to have landed while the other hovered just above the ground. All around them, soldiers could be seen, some clad in black and others in tan, all heavily armored. Only a few stood guard around the perimeter, the remainder busy unloading the landed craft. A few minutes later, Keith heard the sound of trucks and turned to see one driving up to the edge of the woods, now with a heavy machine gun mounted above the cab. This alerted the sentries guarding the landing craft below, but it didn't matter.

The advisors gave the order, and all sides of the valley erupted with the sounds of gunfire. It seemed that they had the Earthers surrounded. Initially, Keith was dizzied by the sudden cacophony. Coming back to his senses, he brought his lever action to his shoulder and fired off a round. The Earthers, nearly 400 meters out, were mere dots along the bottom of the valley. Keith didn't see the point of trying to fire from this distance, but the advisors insisted that the volleys continue none the less. Moments later, a shout went out, and the black shoulders advanced down the valley from all sides. The trucks moved up in between them, firing all the way. Up ahead, Keith could see Gaz's group moving up. Keith stood up to join them but crouched back down when his advisor shouted, "Group 17, hold!"

During the first few minutes, the Earthers below were running about, seemingly scattered. They had since regrouped, and return fire started coming in. Almost immediately, the black shoulders advancing over open ground began dropping, and one of the trucks exploded as a rocket flew out from between the landing craft. There was a snap right beside Keith's head, and he cursed loudly, ducking behind a tree. His group's advisor then started shouting at them to continue firing. With all the courage he could muster, Keith again swung his rifle around the tree, aiming back down into the valley. It appeared that the Earthers had established a perimeter and were beginning to push outward, focusing their fire on groups of black shoulders and forcing them to the ground. The hovering landing craft at the bottom of the valley had also begun to take off, and its front cannon was now firing, tearing men in half.

Just as it seemed that the assault was ready to break, a pair of jets flew in from overhead, strafing the valley. This caused significant casualties among the Earthers. Before they could recover, the jets came around again, strafing the landing craft and causing it to crash to the ground. It then exploded, showering the area with burning fuel and debris. Keith almost laughed aloud. It seemed that they could win this. It was then that he noticed an unusual shape in the corner of his vision. Turning right, he saw a large foliage-covered figure aiming its weapon at the advisor.

"Sir, look out!" Keith's voice nearly cracked as he screamed the words, raising his rifle. Without hesitation, the advisor hit the dirt and rolled. Keith fired squarely into the figure whose only reaction was to aim at Keith. Finding his lever-action empty, Keith threw it to the ground and swung his issued rifle around, firing it wildly and falling backward. Fortunately for him, the other members of Group 17 had realized what was going on and had turned to engage the attacker, peppering it with fire until it finally collapsed. It was not alone, as another one stood up firing, killing two recruits. It then tried to run but was promptly gunned down, one recruit jumping onto its chest and emptying a magazine into its head. By now, the advisor had gotten back up, checking the first figure's body before turning towards Keith, who was lying on his back in shock.

"Good job!" The advisor then waved his hand in the air, shouting, "Group 17! Advance!"

As the other men moved forward, Keith blinked and pulled himself together. Standing up, he walked up to the first figure, pulling aside the foliage. It was an Earther, as massive as he imagined and armored from head to toe. Its chest armor was peppered with bullet strikes, with only a mere few having pierced it. Looking up at its helmet, he saw his reflection in the goggles. Slinging his issued rifle around to his back, he reached forward and grabbed each side of the helmet, pulling it. It took some effort, but after a few long seconds and a hiss of air, the helmet came loose, and he removed it. Much to his surprise, the face looking back up at him was female, eyes glazed over and blood dripping from her lips.

"No, no no no no no!" Keith stumbled backwards. He'd been taught to never as much as slap a woman, and now he'd shot one. "Fuck!"

He turned back towards the battle and shook himself. Dozens of dead and injured recruits littered the hillside, and the screams of the injured filled the air. None the less, all groups, including his own, were closing in on the remaining Earthers. It appeared that they'd be finished soon. His train of thought was then interrupted by the shouts of advisors coming up from behind.

"Move up and rejoin your group!" they shouted. Keith looked over at them and nodded. These advisors had medic markings on their armor and were rapidly tagging everyone they came across as dead or wounded—one less thing for Keith to worry about.

As he ran down the hill, he could see a few Earthers left, fighting back to back between the now wrecked and burning dropships. By the time he reached the bottom, it was finished. An Earther commander was the last to fall, and now the recruits were practically tearing him apart for trophies. All around, the ground was littered with munitions, and many recruits were grabbing as much as they could carry. Meanwhile, the advisors stood by at the edges, checking Earthers' bodies and communicating their findings with each other. Keith promptly began to partake in the looting, grabbing a dead Earther's rifle and stuffing his pockets with magazines and hand grenades.

This feeding frenzy was then interrupted by the advisors, yelling at everyone to get to the tree line. Keith looked up at one of them. This was the first time that he'd heard even a hint of panic from the advisors. Most of the men obeyed and began jogging towards the tree line, but a few groups remained, laughing and packing their pockets with whatever they could find. A moment later, even the advisors turned and ran. At this, Keith got the hint and began running as fast as he could back up the hill.

About a quarter of the way up, he tripped, landing face-first into the grass.

"Damn it, Keith!" a pissed off voice barked.

Keith turned and was surprised to see Gaz lying on the ground behind him.

"Gaz! Gaz, we gotta go!" said Keith.

"Help me up." Gaz sat up. Blood was spattered across his face, and the left side of his pants were soaked with blood.

Keith threw Gaz's arm over his shoulder and did his best to lift him up. Gaz was heavier than expected, but none the less they started back up the hill as fast as they could. As they reached the tree line, Keith was suddenly deafened by a massive shockwave.

Falling to the ground screaming, Keith rolled onto his back to face the valley. What was the battlefield was now a massive cloud of flying rocks and debris shooting hundreds of feet up into the air. Before he could find a moment to breathe, the whole valley erupted again, knocking him back down to the ground. Having lost any semblance of hearing, he slapped Gaz's shoulder and pointed towards the woods. Gaz nodded, and together they got back up as best they could, making a run for the trucks.

Chapter 6 – Victory Day

Having survived their first battle, the recruits celebrated in excess, spurred by numerous barrels of malt liquor supplied by the advisors. Keith was not the only one deafened by the blast, so at the very least, he was able to revel among his deaf brethren, unable to communicate aside from exaggerated toasts and unheard cheers. Gaz spent the following week recovering. As Keith had found out later, Gaz had taken a grenade blast from the left side. Fortunately, for his sake, it was relatively far off. None the less he proceeded to partake in the festivities from his cot, having barely recovered from the anesthesia before being handed a drink. The advisors, as with all things, seemed unaffected. Neither deafened by the blast nor reveling in victory, a few handshakes and high-fives were exchanged before they resumed their usual patrols around the camp.

During this time, it also became apparent that the Unified Dominion Armed Forces were significantly larger than previously thought. As it turned out, most of the recruits attacking from the opposite side of the valley were from another UDAF force. After the battle, they regrouped at the base camp and promptly joined in the festivities. Most of these men came from the ranches up north, a few of which Keith's Echo Ranch had previously fought in territorial disputes. As to where the jets came from, that was still open to question. There was no sign of the jets nor their pilots following the battle.

Two days and a communal hangover later, the recruits were presented with their first paychecks. These were provided in the form of extra rations, bonds for livestock, or Earth Union Credits (despite having separated from the Earth Union some time ago, EUC or "yukes" were still maintained as the primary currency on-world.) The advisors also offered the option to wait on payment until the next "cycle," whatever that meant, and receive compensation from both cycles with interest. Near to none of the recruits chose that option. Keith approached the table with his mind already made up: he'd be taking the livestock bonds. He owned a small plot of land on the Echo Ranch, but it was worthless without animals or crops. Upon arrival, the advisor looked up at Keith, down at his clipboard, then back up to Keith.

"What's your name?"

"Keith. I'm a farmer."

The advisor looked down at his clipboard again. "Keith, please report to the command tent."

"Something wrong?" Keith eyed the advisor suspiciously.

"Everything's alright. A few of us just want to talk to you. Move along."

Keith stepped aside, pissed off about not receiving his payment and anxious about what this meant. None the less, he did as he was told and began the walk across the field.

The command tent was at the northern edge of the field. It was flanked by advisor quarters, large blocky tents that looked sturdier than some ranch houses. Under normal circumstances, the recruits were ordered to stay away from this area, and those that approached found themselves swiftly punished. Soon enough, Keith was stopped by an advisor and was promptly asked his name and reason for being there. When Keith introduced himself, the advisor cut him off, saying, "Ah, Farmboy!" and promptly walked him the rest of the way.

Upon stepping in, Keith was met with a blast of freezing cold air. The interior of the command tent seemed even bigger than it appeared from the outside. The walls were lined with maps and whiteboards, each packed with notes. Desks were scattered throughout, nearly all of them sporting multiple computer screens. Never in his life had Keith seen so much technology in one place. The last time he'd seen a computer was in the boss' office at Echo ranch, and that was not nearly as impressive as the arrays featured here. This was also the first time that he'd seen the advisors without their combat armor. All of them were tall, for the most part surprisingly pale, and muscular beyond belief. Most wore the same thing: olive drab tank tops and baggy, dark green pants. A few men and women in the back wore suits and ties, unexpected and unusual garb for this area. One particularly attractive blonde looked up at Keith and gave him a friendly smile, leaving him dumbstruck until one of the advisors began snapping his fingers.

"Keith, yes?" asked the advisor,

"Yessir."

"Over here, please." The advisor gestured towards a table further in.

Keith walked over and was told to sit down, which he did. There were three men on the other side of the table. To Keith's right was the "new man," intently looking over an electronic notepad. He didn't seem to notice that Keith had entered the tent. To the left and directly in front of Keith were two advisors, their helmets off but otherwise fully armored. The one to the left was darker skinned, with dark hair and young features. The man in the middle looked the oldest and sported short, bleach-blonde hair and pink eyes. The pink eyes confused Keith, but so much about the advisors didn't make sense that he didn't pay it much mind.

"You have a last name?" asked the advisor in the middle.

"Lane."

The "new man" began typing in notes.

"Good to meet you, Mr. Lane. I am Captain Kowal." Kowal then gestured to the advisor next to him. "This is Sergeant Anand. You have already met him, albeit informally."

Keith looked at Anand but didn't recognize him. "You can call me Keith. There a reason that I'm here?"

"We've got a few questions and a potential opportunity for you." Kowal picked up a small note from the table. "You saved Sergeant Anand here in last week's battle. Quick thinking on your part."

"You're the one I told to 'lookout'?" asked Keith, looking at Anand.

"Yes."

"Well, hi." Keith wasn't sure what to say.

Kowal continued. "I also understand that you did well for yourself on the rifle range?"

"Yessir."

Kowal then leaned forward, staring directly at Keith. "So, what do you think of our operations here?"

"Y'all seem to be doing a decent job. We've stopped Earth, I guess we're now bringing Dominion back together?"

Kowal smiled. "One step at a time, there is still work to do with Earth." He looked down at his notes. "Tell me about yourself. Family? Friends? Where are you from?"

"I'm from Echo ranch, daddy's dead. Never got to meet my mother."

"Where was your dad from?"

"He was an Earther if I understand right, he didn't talk about it much though."

"And what did you do at Echo?"

"Protect cattle mostly. Occasionally I worked the fields if we were shorthanded. What's this got to do with anything?"

Kowal smiled again. Keith couldn't tell if it was condescending or warm. "Nothing much. How interested would you be in working alongside us? Being more than just another recruit? Not everyone on Dominion sees us the way you do. Having local talent would improve our image, make our job easier. You understand?"

"Yessir!" Keith didn't, but it sounded good. "So, this like a promotion?"

"More or less."

"I'll take it! What will I be doing?"

"Excellent! If you could please follow Anand here, we just have some small things to take care of. We also need to get your pay in order."

At another table, Anand helped Keith fill out more paperwork. Like Kowal earlier, Anand asked a lot of questions about what Keith did prior to joining the Unified Dominion Armed Forces. It seemed unproductive for the most part, and the process dragged on for nearly an hour. The fact the Keith could not read did not help. Once everything was finished up, the agreement on Keith's pay was finalized, with a bonus. At that, Anand finally let him go. More training was not an appealing prospect to Keith, but at the very least, Anand gave him the rest of the day off. So, Keith stepped out of the command tent, happy to have been promoted but not sure what he had gained, nor what exactly it entailed.

As he walked back across the field, he was blasted with a gust of hot wind. He couldn't decide if it was better or worse than the freezing temperatures within the tent. As soon he reached the mess tent, he sat down at a table across from Gaz, who was busy peeling open a package of fresh bandages.

"How you doin' Keith?" asked Gaz, looking up from the olive drab plastic.

"I just got promoted!"

Gaz appeared confused. "Wait. What?"

44

"The advisors gave me a bonus and have signed me up for extra training. I got to go into the command tent."

At this, Gaz put down the bandages and checked over his shoulder before returning his focus to Keith. "So, what they got in there?"

"Lots of computers, maps. They are even wearing ties in there! A few ladies too."

"What was on the maps?"

Now Keith eyed Gaz, confused. "I couldn't tell, honestly. There was a local roadmap, but also a bunch of others I didn't recognize."

"Mhm." Gaz seemed lost in thought. "And you said ties, like suits and ties?"

"Yessir."

Now Gaz bore a more serious expression. Keith stared back, unnerved.

Finally, Gaz exhaled and said, "Well, congratulations on the promotion!" He reached out and shook Keith's hand, leaving a smear of blood on it. "Fuck. Sorry."

"It's alright." Keith began wiping his hand off on his pant leg.

"So, what are they going to have you doing?"

"Dunno yet, I start tomorrow. Guess I'll know then!"

"Yes, I suppose you will."

The next day, Keith was introduced to the other recruits that had been promoted. Like Keith, each had performed an action that the advisors looked upon favorably. Rather than partaking in the usual maneuvers, they were taken aside and briefed on what they would be doing. Starting out at least, they'd be serving as assistants to their assigned advisors. This new role would be taken on immediately, and they were now expected to report directly to their advisors instead of their former units. Lastly, each was given a radio, pre-programmed and ready to go. The radio was part of their new position – lose the radio, lose the promotion.

They were then brought to the firing range, where they were issued new rifles and promptly taught how to operate them. The externals were made of a dark green polymer, with the magazine located behind the grip. Overall, this proved to be the hardest part to master, as Keith found himself repeatedly fumbling his rifle as he tried to find the magazine catch. At least, unlike the guns issued out to the rest of the recruits, these rifles appeared to be brand new. They were also far more accurate, which satisfied Keith greatly. Though the other promoted were older than Keith, they were not necessarily wiser. Within the first hour, the advisors kicked out one of them for waving his new rifle about carelessly. He did not get to keep it. From then on, Keith and the others made a point of staying in line.

That evening Keith returned to the mess tent, tired, but happy to have not been running around all day. Gaz, on the other hand, had been running around, partaking in the usual formations of lines and advances. He sat down at the table, drenched with sweat and mildly sunburned as always. On the upside, he seemed to be losing weight. Today, he asked fewer questions but was all ears none the less. A few minutes in, Keith placed his new rifle on the table, showing it off. Gaz proceeded to look over the gun thoroughly, running his finger along the markings on the sides.

"Valkyrie Arms, I'm not familiar with that brand."

"That's what those letters are on the side?" asked Keith.

"Yes, sir." Gaz picked it up and looked down the sights. "This is nice, definitely take care of it."

"Will do. It's accurate as hell too."

"Can't say I was ever much of a marksman." Gaz smiled. "Seems you're moving up in the world."

"A little bit at a time. Hope my plot's doing alright. The boss at Echo is probably pretty pissed about me disappearing on him."

Gaz chuckled. "Yeah, I'd imagine. I've been meaning to get back in contact with Belcher Ranch. There are people back there waiting on me."

"Family?"

"Not exactly."

Keith nodded. "Same."

"Y'know, depending on your situation, UDAF may be a great opportunity for you. Seems to be room to move up."

"I'm thinking about it. We'll see where it goes."

"Well, whatever you do," Gaz leaned back. "Definitely keep me posted on what's going on. You're doing well for yourself."

"Yessir!"

Chapter 7 - Tempest

Earth Union Drop Ship Bestir 7 "Bold Lola"

The back of Sergeant Dan Felman's helmet bumped against his seat's headrest as the drop ship entered Dominion's atmosphere. The walls had already started to shake, being nearly drowned out by the rattle of twenty-four other sets of body armor. Earth Union dropships were large U-shaped craft. Each carried a full platoon: twenty-five men in each "arm" with an armored vehicle suspended outside the craft in between. Capacity totaled fifty men, not including the vehicle and drop ship crews. Due to their size, they were only permitted to fly by the brute force of their thrusters as opposed to some miracle in aerodynamics. To the inexperienced, it felt like Lola was going to break apart under her own weight.

Looking to the right, Felman smirked at the fresh recruits holding on to their crash seats for dear life. This was his seventh combat drop, not including his training with airborne regiments. The recruits here, on the other hand, were ground pounders: regular army that had never done this before and would probably never do this again. Looking left, he could see the air-crewman in his seat, eyeing up the rows of troops ahead of him. He was probably visually double-checking each and every one of their harnesses, not that he could do anything about it at this point. Facing back forward, Felman turned a laminated map around in his hands, focusing on it through the constant shaking and dim red light. It was a topological map of the Landing Zone and the surrounding area. Forested, hilly terrain surrounded the LZ. The idea was that it would help keep the locals away, not that it did much for the last landing group.

"Studying for a test?" Felman heard through his comms.

He looked up at his spotter, Specialist Jaime Loesche, who was sitting across from him. "Good to freshen up."

"Yeah, you're right." Loesche leaned forward a bit. "Someone's gotta be an overachiever."

"Better to be one in this case," replied Felman, flipping the map over. Across the back, he had a series of notes written down regarding local flora and fauna. He hadn't been to Dominion before, and he wasn't going to end his military career by stepping on something he shouldn't. "Check out this shit." He tapped the back of the map. "Spike leaf: 'Bone-like leaves have a coating of fiberglass-like particles. Injuries from spike leaf are exacerbated by this material and will not heal without medical attention.'"

Loesche shook his head. "Can't be as bad as Acacia trees."

"You're right there."

Suddenly the entire ship seemed to bounce, followed by a chorus of shouts from the recruits. Over the rumble, gagging could be heard. Almost immediately, the flight crewman to Felman's left raised his hand and shouted, "Whatever you bastards do, *do not* fucking throw up on *my* ship!" He enunciated the words in a way that made Felman chuckle.

Turning back to Loesche, Felman then said, "My money's on the fat one."

"Nope, the corporal three seats down."

"Double if my guy rips off his mask."

"You're on!"

Fifteen minutes later, the ship shuttered again as it switched from free fall to controlled flight. At this point, the crewman undid his restraints and started walking down the aisle, keying his helmet mic into the overhead speakers.

"We will be landing in ten minutes! Ten minutes! Do not undo your restraints!" The crewman slapped the hand of a recruit who was fiddling with the buckles on his seat. "Check your equipment! Greenlight in ten minutes!"

Felman unlocked his sniper rifle from the bracket next to his seat, opening the bolt to confirm that there was a cartridge in the chamber. Loesche did the same. His was one of the new assault rifles that weren't yet standard issue.

"No vomit," observed Felman, looking back down the line.

"Game's rigged, man." Loesche finished checking his weapon then paused. "I still can't believe last recon group got wiped out, like what the fuck?"

"It's unusual how coordinated these locals are." Felman closed the bolt on his rifle. "Anyhow, that's why we're here."

Loesche nodded.

Soon enough, the lights turned green, and the crewman again got up from his seat to begin barking at everyone to stand up. Coming to their feet, some recruits lost their footing and fell back into their seats or onto other recruits, unable to maintain their balance in the constantly shifting cabin. Most combat drops were like this outside of marine and airborne units, so Felman and Loesche were more amused than anything else. The flight crewman, of course, was not. About a minute later, the rear doors dropped with a bang, and everyone inside piled out into the light of the bright Dominion sun.

Chapter 8 – Gileppo

Keith stood in line, this time in front of his group. That morning training had been called off, and everyone was ordered to ready themselves. Again, Keith found himself with a familiar feeling of existential dread in the pit of his stomach. Round two against Earth. He looked up at Advisor Anand, who was approaching him.

"Good morning, sir!"

Anand stared back, coldly. "Inspect your group and report."

"Yessir."

It had been a week since Keith's promotion, and relatively speaking, he was doing well for himself. Two others had since been kicked out of their new positions, one proving to have been dumb as a rock, while the other was simply ill-motivated. The rest had since been assigned to advisors, many of whom seemed enthusiastic about training their new assistants. Keith had been assigned to Advisor Anand, who seemed to just deal with it.

As Keith walked along the line, he nodded at one of the new recruits. Marco was from Echo Ranch as well, having arrived after the battle in the valley. It was nice to see a familiar face, even more so one that was more motivated than average. Since the last battle, replacements had been brought in to make up for losses. Group 17 had lost four guys. One had died early, hit on the hill overlooking the landing zone. Two were killed by the Earthers in the brush. The fourth had been hit during the advance and was too injured to continue serving.

Having found Group 17's gear to be in order, Keith returned to the front and again stood at attention. "Advisor Anand, Group 17 is in order!"

"Good." Anand turned so that his back was facing Keith and stood at attention, signaling the other advisors that his group was ready.

No longer under Anand's gaze, Keith relaxed a little. Being under Anand's purview, combined with news from Marco, had left Keith on edge. As was expected, the foreman at Echo was less than happy about Keith's sudden disappearance. But a deal was a deal, and Keith's plot was still safe, for now. According to Marco, it'd be in Keith's best interests to return to Echo to, if nothing else, inform the ranch owner that he was still alive and would be coming back eventually.

Soon enough, the rumble of engines could be heard, but rather than the usual column, they were greeted with a line of damaged and smoking vehicles. As the line slowed to a stop, the engine compartment of one truck burst into flames. It then rolled into the vehicle ahead of it with a metallic crunch. Almost immediately, groups of advisors ran towards the column, medical bags in hand. Keith and most of the other recruits just stared at the scene dumbfounded, at least until the advisors began shouting at them to help.

At this, Keith ran to one of the closest trucks. Coming around to the back of it, he watched as an injured advisor was pulled out. The advisor was missing his right arm from the elbow down and was covered in his own blood. Keith reached forward to grab him but was promptly pushed aside and told to help with the injured recruits. Looking into the bed, Keith was met with a pile of bloodied and burned bodies. Some were still alive. Most were not. Those that could help themselves began shuffling their way out the back of the truck. Meanwhile, Keith and members of his group began pulling out those who couldn't.

"Live ones to the mess tent, dead ones along the road! Pick it up!" shouted an advisor, clapping his hands as he approached.

By now, Keith and another recruit were in the back of the truck, doing their best to carry out one of the broken bodies. This one had lost both legs below the knee and was covered in burns. Within minutes, they'd deposited the body next to the road and had returned for another. The next man they pulled out was still alive, though both his legs were peppered with shrapnel.

"Shit man! How'd this happen?" asked Keith, starting to pick up the injured recruit.

"Incendiaries just started raining on us…" The recruit spoke with the heavy Italian accent common among the northern ranches.

"Geez man!"

By now, Keith had started lowering the recruit down onto a stretcher that two other men had positioned behind the truck. Despite his arms straining under the weight, Keith did his best to let the injured man down gently. His efforts were then interrupted by the sound of gunfire erupting from the camp.

Jerking his head right, Keith was surprised to see several recruits aiming skyward. Redirecting his attention up, Keith spotted a steel-colored disc, a meter in diameter, hovering maybe a hundred meters above them. Instinctively, Keith reached for his rifle, only to hear Anand shouting at him over the radio to stop his men from firing. Nodding to himself, Keith let his rifle hang loosely from its sling and began waving his arms at the other recruits, trying to explain over the din that the advisors wanted them to stop. Not a moment later, a rocket shot up from the back edge of the camp and exploded next to the flying disk, showering the column of trucks with shards of metal and plastic. Keith and those around him stared at the puff of smoke where the disc used to be. Others began to cheer, waving their fists in the air or kicking components that had fallen to the ground around them.

"Farmboy!"

Keith snapped to attention, looking towards the source of the voice. Anand was walking towards him quickly.

"With me!" he shouted, signaling Keith to follow him.

"Yessir!" Keith glanced at the other recruit that had been helping him move bodies and shrugged before hopping down. He had to move quickly to catch up with Anand, who was already headed in the opposite direction towards the command tent.

"Sorry sir, I couldn't get them to stop-"

"Don't worry about it. You're doing fine," interrupted Anand, without looking at Keith.

Halfway through the field, Keith observed two other advisors, one with a still smoking missile launcher over his shoulder.

"They've found us," said the advisor with the missile launcher.

"Yup. Let's get this shit packed up. We don't have much time," answered the other.

By now, Keith and Anand had reached the command tent, where other advisors and their assistants were gathering. In the middle of the group stood Captain Kowal, his helmet under his arm. Keith immediately began trying to wipe the smeared blood off his arms, vest, and pants, until he realized that the other recruits were in a similar state. So, he snapped to attention and waited. Anand, on the other hand, stood a little straighter, but otherwise maintained the same stance. A few minutes later, when all the squad leaders had gathered, Kowal began to speak.

"Sergeants, start packing up the camp. We need to be out of here, ASAP." Kowal then glanced at Keith and the other recruits present. "Have your assistants gather your squads and prepare to move out. Set your radios to the alternate channel. We'll be reinforcing the Gileppo Ranch."

All the advisors nodded. Without another word, Kowal turned and left the group, walking back to the command tent. Outside it, Keith could see two men in unfamiliar black uniforms, waiting for him.

"Farmboy!"

"Yessir!" Keith's attention snapped back to Anand.

"Give me your radio."

58

Keith nodded, pulling his radio out of its pouch and handing it to Anand.

Anand turned on the radio, pressing a few buttons before handing it back to Keith. "Gather the squad, find a truck that works. Radio me when you've done that. Got it?"

"Yessir!" Keith nodded.

Keith glanced back at the command tent, but Kowal and the two men had already disappeared back inside it.

Returning to the rabble surrounding the trucks, Keith spotted Marco, who was dragging another body to the side of the road.

"Hey! Marco!" he shouted.

"Ciao!" Marco finished laying the body down and looked up at Keith.

"Do me a favor, find a truck that works. I'll be getting our group together."

"You got it!" Immediately, Marco began running along the line of trucks, hopping in the cab of each to inspect them.

Keith then began waving his arms wide, shouting, "Group 17! On me!" Soon enough, he'd gathered all but one of his guys and proceeded towards a truck that Marco had laid claim to. Upon reaching it, Keith radioed his status to Anand, who arrived a few minutes later.

"Who is missing, exactly?" asked Anand, climbing into the back of the truck.

"I think his name is Alejandro, sir."

By now, other groups were getting themselves in order, climbing into still-functioning trucks or lining up beside the road. Turning towards this scene, Anand bellowed, "Alejandro! Where the fuck are you!?"

Almost immediately, a recruit immerged from the horde, approaching the back of the truck. "Here!"

Anand grabbed the front of Alejandro's vest, lifting him into the back of the truck with one arm and slamming him into the bench seat. "If I am not present, you listen to him!" shouted Anand, pointing back at Keith. "Got it?"

Alejandro nodded. Keith watched wide-eyed.

It was about mid-afternoon when they arrived at the Gileppo Ranch. Prior to this, Gileppo had been a direct competitor with Keith's Echo Ranch to the south. Keith had fought in two of the border conflicts between Gileppo and Echo, though "fought" was a relative term. Fortunately, for his sake, both disputes were settled by shouting and waving weapons around. It was uncommon for them to turn into full-fledged firefights. None the less, Keith had always been curious about what the Gileppo Ranch looked like, though perhaps it would have been more interesting before today.

The fields surrounding the ranch houses and barns were pockmarked with burnt craters. Around the craters, several cattle carcasses baked in the sun, the remains of their enclosures collapsed around them. Despite all this, the ranch structures were nearly untouched. Aside from the scrapes of shrapnel, it appeared that none had been hit directly. All around them and scattered throughout the yard were hundreds of scraps of paper. Keith stared at the scene for a moment as the truck slowed to a halt. It didn't make any sense.

"Everybody out!" ordered Anand.

Keith was one of the first out, dropping to the dusty ground behind the truck. Bending down, Keith picked up a piece of paper, trying to decipher the text on it.

"Put that down."

Keith looked over at Anand, and without a second thought, dropped it. It wasn't like he'd be able to read it anyway.

Almost immediately, Keith and his group were ordered to reinforce the north edge of the ranch's fields. Here, a series of earthen fortifications had already been dug. A few advisors walked along the top of them,

61

monitoring the edge of the tree line to the north through binoculars or double-checking the makeshift bunkers. Other UDAF recruits were scattered throughout earthworks, trying to find or make some meager shade in the exposed trenches. Nearly all of them were covered in dirt, and as Keith approached, he could see that many of them were bleeding from the ears.

Anand reached the line first, signaling Keith and the rest of Group 17 to stop. As he began coordinating with another advisor, Keith looked over the positions ahead of him. There were two thin trenches, spaced about 10 meters apart and connected by multiple smaller paths. The sharp edges of the trench walls were periodically cut by blast craters, some of which had since been dug deeper to expand the line. Bloodied bandages littered the area, and a broken stretcher lay a few feet away. Despite all the apparent recent activity, there was not a single spent shell to be seen. Keith's attention was then drawn back to the ranch houses by the sound of shouting. Turning to face them, Keith watched as a man in a white jacket with suitcases under each arm stormed out of the largest house, shouting at every advisor within earshot. The rant was a mix of Spanish, Italian, and English, strung together into a barely coherent storm of insults.

By now, the commotion had attracted the attention of Marco and the rest of Group 17, most of whom watched in amusement.

"Ol' man Gileppo's getting kicked out!" said Marco, elbowing Keith.

Keith watched as the old man proceeded to get into the face of one of the advisors. The advisor was stepping backward with his hands up, trying to diffuse whatever situation was unfolding. However, the old man was having none of it, even going as far as slapping the advisor's armored faceplate.

"I can't imagine he's too happy about the holes in his fields," said another recruit, making everyone chuckle.

"No, not at all," answered Keith.

Having hurt his hand on the advisor's face, Gileppo's wrath subsided, giving way to glaring and slurs under his breath. This made Keith laugh. Echo's biggest competitor had been reduced to shambles, and with no effort on his part. One less thing to worry about when he finally got to go home.

"Farmboy!"

"Yessir!" Keith's attention snapped back to Anand.

"Grab four guys and set up on the western side." Anand pointed down the trench line to Keith's left. "Find what tools you can, reinforce the trench, and keep your eyes open."

"You got it."

Without another word, Anand signaled the other half of Group 17, including Marco, and proceeded to the closest ramp into the trenches. Keith followed suit, waving the remaining four members to follow him. They walked along the tops of the lines about three-quarters of the way before proceeding down a ramp. Once in, Keith and his group received no shortage of dirty looks from the recruits already present. Judging by their dialect, they likely belonged to the Gileppo ranch and recognized Keith as an outsider.

Nonetheless, Keith made it through, and they were soon positioned in a crater at the front of the line. To the dismay of his men, Keith immediately ordered that they start digging. Keith partook as well, though. He couldn't bear to stand around while others were working. An hour in, a group of advisors came around handing out rations. It was a welcome relief. Not only were they starving, but it was also an excuse to stop digging.

Tired of the trench, Keith hopped up onto the grassy ground in front of it, sitting down cross-legged as he tore into his ration pack. Chewing on a biscuit, he stared for a few minutes at the white tree line. Beyond the fields were open woods. Not a lot of low growth, so he could see reasonably far in. No sign of the Earthers. Swallowing the biscuit, he tore open another bag of what was supposed to be stew. Turning back towards the ranch houses, he watched as the old man once more accosted the advisors. He had since packed everything he could into the back of a truck, his family included. A few minutes later, ol' man Gilleppo was driving away down the road. Many of his ranch hands followed on foot, strapping everything they could to their backs. Soon only a few remained, staring at the armored vehicles that the advisors had since brought in.

There were three of them. Each had six wheels and a turret, out of which protruded a thin, square-shaped barrel. One had positioned itself roughly in the middle of the property, behind the largest of the barns. The other two set up in the woods on either side, camouflaging themselves with brown nets. At some point, he wanted to get a closer look at one. Anything with an engine was exciting to him, and these were among the largest vehicles that he had seen.

Redirecting his focus down the line, Keith could see Gaz at the other end. Gaz was also sitting on the grass outside the trenches, though he looked exhausted. Drenched in sweat, he began stripping off his armored vest and field jacket. Nearby, two advisors watched in dismay, though they didn't say anything. It was early summer, and the sun was beating down hard. The lack of shade certainly wasn't helping

"Recruit."

Keith was startled by the sudden presence of the advisor, standing a few feet away from him. Keith looked up at him.

"Best you get back in the trench. You're exposed up here."

Keith nodded, gathered his things, and climbed back down into the crater.

Chapter 9 – Drum Run

Keith sat in the crater, his back up against the wall, staring up at the darkening sky. The sky itself was a tarnished gold, and a thick bronze haze had set in. A few feet away, two of Keith's men threw pebbles at a can. The other two lay asleep on the other side of the crater. Having finished repairs and improvements to the line, they'd spent the last few hours waiting. For what, they weren't sure. But it sure as hell wasn't interesting. At the very least, the setting sun had brought the temperature down, which was a welcome change of pace. Keith exhaled. He was close to falling asleep as well.

Suddenly, one of the sleeping men opened his eyes and asked, "Do you feel that?"

Keith looked down at him, confused. "What?"

The recruit was now partially upright, one hand flat on the ground with the other against the crater wall.

Following suit, Keith placed his left hand on the ground. After a few seconds, he could feel it too.

"What the…?"

The ground was shaking. Though it was barely distinguishable from the breeze, a low rumble could be heard.

Reaching to his right, Keith grabbed his rifle and checked to make sure it was loaded. By now, the two recruits throwing pebbles had gotten the idea and grabbed their weapons as well, peering out over the wall. One recruit still lay asleep.

"Wake him up!" whispered Keith.

They shook the shoulder of the still sleeping man who woke up with a start. Upon seeing everyone else on alert, he promptly came to his feet.

"Fucking aye! I need to piss," he mumbled, after collecting his kit.

Anand's voice then came over Keith's radio, "Keith, ready your men. Hold your fire until I say so."

"Yessir!" Keith answered, passing the word along a moment later.

He then stood up and looked out over the fields ahead of them. The tree line was now black against the setting sun, and he could not see far into the darkening haze. Over the next few minutes, the rumble steadily grew until the first dark figures appeared. They were large, definitely vehicles. Almost immediately, a few pops could be heard through the line as recruits fired. This was immediately followed by advisors shouting at them to stop. One of the shapes returned fire, peppering a position with an automatic cannon. The electric buzz of a rail gun then echoed from behind the line as one of the advisor vehicles fired, striking the figure which immediately ground to a halt.

As they approached the edge of the tree line, Keith was finally able to make them out. Most of them looked like automated tractors, except these had gun turrets. Among the drones, full-sized tanks appeared, maybe one for every half-dozen. One of them opened fire, razing one of the barns. The advisor vehicles fired back, and the front of the closest tank seemed to erupt. A moment later, it emerged from the smoke seemingly unscathed and fired again, blasting the wheel off the nearest advisor vehicle.

It was then that Keith's men opened fire, not that it did anything. When Keith found himself unable to persuade them to stop, he radioed Anand.

"Advisor, sir, we can't hurt these things. Orders!?"

"Hold your fire and stand by," Anand responded dryly.

"Fuck!" Keith cursed aloud. Peering over the top of the wall, he watched helplessly as half a dozen more tracked drones and a tank rolled into the field, impervious to their small arms.

Suddenly the front of the tank tipped forward, nose-diving into the ground and packing its barrel with dirt. At the other end of the field, a drone tipped, this time sideways as the earth gave way underneath it. It appeared that there were several pitfall traps hidden throughout the field.

"Haha! Screw you!" one of Keith's men shouted, flipping off the now helpless tank.

Not a moment later, another one pulled around, driving past the first tank and opening fire with its machine guns.

"Jesus!" They all ducked as shots pelted the earth around them. When the fire subsided, they popped up again, taking potshots at the approaching juggernaut.

The Earthers were halfway across the field now. Among the drones more tanks appeared, each taking turns blasting defensive positions or leveling the ranch houses. The drones, for the most part, focused their fire on the recruits trying to return fire. The shots that found their mark blew recruits to pieces, quickly persuading the remainder to duck. Suddenly, part of the field erupted, knocking a drone on its side and completely shattering another. Another blast followed, this one directly underneath a tank, blowing off its tracks and wheels on both sides. It seemed the advisors had rigged half the field to blow.

Keith again peered over the top of the wall, equally dumbfounded and deafened by the blasts. Burning debris was still falling to the ground among the drones and tanks. Though most of them were still firing, nearly all had stopped advancing. A few long minutes later, they began to back up towards the tree line.

As the din subsided, Keith looked to his left and right at his men. "Is everyone alright?" he asked, barely able to hear his own voice.

The man to his left nodded. His helmet was scraped by a close shot, but he was otherwise uninjured. The recruits to his right also nodded.

Farther to the left, Keith heard a voice cursing. Turning back in that direction, Keith observed that the fourth recruit in his team had thoroughly wet himself at some point during the engagement.

"Piss off!" said the recruit, seeing Keith's expression.

"I believe you've got that covered," answered another recruit, smirking.

Hearing traffic from his radio, Keith began fumbling through the pouches on his vest. Finally, he retrieved it, and pressing the mic button, asked, "Come again, sir?"

Before Anand could repeat his message, a loud buzz filled the air, and the night sky was illuminated with strings of white fire. The first struck the man to Keith's right, turning him to vapor and spraying the rest of the group with mud and gore. Keith fell down in shock, having to protect his face from the whirlwind of sand and rocks being kicked up around him. The beam then moved away from him down the line, mulching everything in its path.

At the other end of the earthworks, two more beams had appeared, emanating from an unknown source in the skies across the field. Panic spread almost immediately through the recruits. While most were driven to the floors of their trenches, others climbed out, running in random directions in a futile attempt to escape. The beams promptly followed, cutting them down with cold efficiency. Missiles came next, engulfing large sections of the line in fiery blasts. Within seconds even the advisors could no longer keep their heads up.

"Alright, who's still here?" asked Keith over the roar of explosives. He'd finally got himself back together and was now recounting the steps that the advisors repeated over and over. 'Calm yourself, regroup, report to your advisor.' He sat up partially, removing his bleeding arms from around his face.

"Who's still here!?" he shouted.

Down the line, there was a stain where one of his men used to be. Just past it, another lay slumped against the trench wall with significant portions of his torso missing. Turning his head around, he could see one crawling his way towards him. Where the fourth was, Keith did not know. Realizing that the radio was still in his hand, he keyed it.

"Sir, orders!"

After a few moments, he keyed it again.

"Advisor, sir! What should we do!?"

Finally, he received a response, but it was Marco's voice on the other end.

"Keith! Anand's hit, this shit's wacked!"

"Wait, what!?"

"We're fucked!"

Keith's hands were shaking now, and he was starting to hyperventilate. Realizing this, he took a few rushed deep breaths before returning his focus to the radio.

"Where are you!?" shouted Keith into the mic.

"Middle of the trenches, maybe a little bit west," answered Marco.

"We're coming there, wait for us!"

Another explosion went off nearby, showering Keith and the other recruit with dirt. After wiping himself off, Keith sifted through the soil around him until he found his rifle. Pulling it up to his chest, he got up and peered over the top of the trench. The Earth Union had restarted its advance. Throughout the flaming fields and smoke, numerous drones appeared, firing all their weapons. The tanks were also moving forward, the rumble of their guns distinct in the chaos.

"Alright, come on! We gotta go!" shouted Keith, ducking and pulling the one remaining recruit behind him. He could barely hear himself speak.

As they began their run through the trenches, it quickly became apparent that the entire line was in disarray. For every advisor or man with a cool head, there were a dozen recruits in hysterics. Most weren't even bothering to fire at the advancing Earthers. Instead, many were trying to get to some other vague point in the line. Like Keith, what exactly they were trying to accomplish was unclear. The moon was not out, and the explosions and flashes of rifle fire left Keith blind in the stretches of darkness in between. So, he navigated as best he could by feel. When he wasn't being knocked down by other fleeing recruits, Keith was pushing his own way through. One man he assumed was dead screamed in agony as he and the other recruit stumbled over him. Keith just continued forward in a daze.

After what felt like an eternity, Keith finally reached Marco and the remainder of the group. Anand was laid out on the ground, one recruit trying to work on him. Another had his back against the trench wall, white-knuckling his rifle. Marco, on the other hand, was firing wildly at the approaching drones, his expression angry. Blood dripped down his left arm, the result of some sort of hand injury. Keith reached him as he ducked down to reload.

"Marco!"

"Yeah?" Marco cupped his ear towards Keith.

"Where's everyone else?"

To this, Marco gestured down the trench line. About ten feet away lay a pile of dead bodies.

Keith stared at this for a moment before coming back to his senses, focusing his attention on Marco. "We gotta go!"

A nearby blast suddenly forced Keith and everyone else to the trench floor. A few seconds later, they were back on their feet.

"Grab the advisor, let's go!"

Marco and another recruit immediately set to it, cursing Anand's name as they worked to lift his heavy body. Nonetheless, they managed, and soon they were working their way down one of the connections to the rear trench.

It was apparent that whatever was left of the defense had become a rout. The few advisors they encountered were now operating in their own groups. Keith attempted to inform them of Anand's status, but he rapidly found himself unable to get within earshot or flat out being ignored. Eventually, Keith stopped trying and returned to his group. Given the current situation, it was a waste of time that he did not have. Soon enough, they'd exited the rear trench and began their run across the field. Most of the advisor vehicles here were burning. Any that weren't had either left already or were rapidly backing out.

"Which way!?" shouted Marco over the din.

Squinting through the darkness and flashes of light from explosions, Keith finally got his bearing.

"There! Go!" Keith shouted, waving his hand, and they turned to make a run for the tree line.

Chapter 10 – Outreach

Earth Union Landing Zone

Felman stepped out of his tent, stretching as he closed the zipper behind him. The sky was a brightening bronze, the sun having not yet come up over the tree line. He was wearing his base uniform, a navy-blue cotton coverall with an integrated belt around the waist and a flak jacket over it. Looking to the right, he eyed Loesche, who was staring at the ground and smoking a cigarette.

"Still got that headache?" asked Felman.

"Yeah," answered Loesche, exhaling smoke.

"Gravity on Earth is heavier than Mars', and Dominion's is heavier than Earth's."

"…and that's why the Doms are so fucking short." Loesche took one more pull of his cigarette before dropping and stamping it out. "You get any of those crawlers in your tent?"

"Which ones?"

"The flat, spider things."

"None of those."

"Fucking aye!" Loesche suddenly kicked up his right boot. "I keep thinking I'm feeling something!"

"If it makes you feel better, they're harmless. They eat dead skin, mostly."

"No, it doesn't." Loesche looked up at the sky. "No amount of painkiller's gonna make this headache go away."

"Give it time." Felman slapped Loesche's shoulder. "Let's get a move on."

Loesche nodded. "Yep."

Since their arrival a week earlier, most of the low growth around the LZ had been reduced to a pulp. Patches of sand took up everything in between and were quickly adopted as paths. Surrounding the landing zone were mostly white-skinned trees with thin, brown leaves. Their thick barks were shell-like, and it was taking the engineers forever to knock them down. Their most recent attempt involved using light explosives, which seemed to be working. Their first try at this had the added effect of freaking out the sentries, who no one had bothered to notify prior. Since then, they'd taken to scheduling demolitions.

The perimeter of the LZ was expanding into the surrounding woods faster than the engineers could keep up. In the middle, there was barely enough room for two dropships to land simultaneously. The pilots managed to despite this, the landings running day and night. As a result, the surrounding area was packed with more crates and vehicles than the men on the ground could deal with. With any luck, the next batch of deliveries would be construction equipment instead of tanks. That, of course, was assuming that the logistics boys on the carrier were paying attention to requests from the ground, which they seldom did. Felman and Loesche paused for a moment as a main battle tank rolled by, its sides adorned with blue Asatru runes and a deer skull strapped to the gun mantlet. Felman watched in amusement.

"So, that's what the Terrans are into these days."

"Not exactly great camouflage," added Loesche, rubbing his temples.

A few minutes later, they reached the command post on the south side of the LZ. Having an excess of large logistics crates, the field commander had the CP built out of them. Each wall was composed of them, stacked two crates high, with a tarp stretched in-between to form a roof. Despite its ludicrous appearance, it provided significantly better protection from small arms fire than a tent with sandbags could have – and it was certainly needed. Twice the landing zone had been attacked since they'd landed here, with periodic sniper fire keeping them on their toes since.

Both Felman and Loesche saluted as they entered, then standing at attention as they waited for the company commander to finish his conversation with a lieutenant. They were discussing the Earth Union assault to the south that took place the day before – an operation that Felman and Loesche did not partake in. In the interest of "hearts and minds," pamphlets had been air-dropped beforehand. When that didn't work, artillery was used, and ground forces were ordered to hold fire until fired upon, attempting to scare the defenders into submission. Thankfully, for the sake of the tank crews, Captain Healy gave the fire-free order only a few minutes in. Soon enough, the conversation was concluded, and the Captain waved Felman and Loesche over.

"Good morning, Captain," said Loesche as they stepped up.

"Good morning, Specialist," Captain Healy answered. "Martian?"

It was an unnecessary question. Felman and Loesche both had markings on their uniforms delineating that alongside their distinct, soft-spoken Mars-Deutsch accents.

"Yes sir."

"Hm." The Captain stared at them for a moment. "You two are here as intelligence, yes?"

"Yes sir," answered Felman. "There was a bit of confusion as to which company we were to be assigned to.

Ultimately, our job is to identify who's coordinating the natives."

"I see, and what will you be needing?" There was a tinge of annoyance in the Captain's voice.

"The carrier was supposed to send a gunship down for us-"

"That should be arriving today," interrupted a man in the back of the post.

At this, both Captain Healy and Sergeant Felman turned to glare at the logistics officer, who apologized before shrinking back to his corner.

"Alright." Sergeant Felman took a breath. "If you could also lend us a squad of your best men, that'd be appreciated, in case we get caught up somewhere."

"No such thing as 'best' men, Sergeant. All these boys are fresh out of basic. We'll see what we can find, but this division is all we've got."

"A division, to invade a planet?" Felman looked confused.

"Aye. According to Central, 'The people of Dominion will gladly flock to the open arms of the Earth Union.' Lotta good that did us. We tried reaching out to the city north of here, didn't turn out so well. They're blaming us for a communications blackout. Not our fault that their infrastructure's shoddy."

"Wait." Felman's expression turned to a scowl. "Central's in charge of this? What happened to Independent Command?"

"The politicians decided that they could run this show. I don't think IC was notified until we were underway." Healy looked down at the map table for a moment and sighed. "Figures that the moment the UK joins up, the Earth Union would start another war." His Irish accent grew heavier. "Then, they'd find another front, just to find an excuse to send us somewhere." He looked up at Felman and Loesche. "I'm sure you Martians know the value of independence."

"Not my place to comment, sir."

Captain Healy nodded. "I'll scratch up something for you two." He picked up a tablet and handed it to Felman. "Until then, brush up on those maps. The higher-ups think they've located the airfield where those planes are coming from. You're both dismissed."

"Yes sir."

Felman and Loesche saluted, then exited the command post. Once they were out of earshot, Loesche turned to Felman, visibly perturbed.

"What is Central thinking? Is this some sort of joke?" Loesche had switched to full Mars-Deutsch.

"Central's never been known for their great minds." Felman answered, also in Deutsch. "You have a cigarette?"

Loesche pulled one out of a pocket on his flak jacket, handing it to Felman and promptly lighting it. Felman took a long pull.

"Furthermore, Mars has only agreed to joint operations under IC's control," said Felman, exhaling smoke. "We shouldn't even be here."

"Fuck." Loesche rubbed his temples with his right hand. "This ought to be a fun ride."

"That's one way to phrase it."

Chapter 11 – Echo

Keith trudged through the low growth painfully, followed closely by Marco and another recruit carrying Anand. The other two recruits trailed behind, eyeing the woods around them suspiciously. Everyone was dehydrated and starving. They'd spent the better part of the night making their way through the woods almost entirely by feel. Having picked their way through brambles and patches of spike leaf, all of them were covered in painful abrasions. The one time they attempted to stop, they found themselves in a Sandjack nest and had to vacate the area quickly. Though Sandjacks were only the size of softballs, the acidic spray they used as a defense was potent. Keith winced as another branch rubbed across a chemical burn on his left arm. It was starting to bleed.

"How much farther?" asked Marco, grunting as he reestablished his hold on Anand.

"We're almost there!" Keith squinted, looking as far as he could through the trees ahead of him. "I think we're almost there."

The other recruit carrying Anand then spoke up. "Why are we still carrying this guy? Isn't he dead?"

"Fuck!" Keith cursed aloud. "He's our advisor, and we're going to see him through this. Anyways, he might still be alive."

"Right." The recruit then let go of Anand, who promptly flopped to the ground despite Marco's efforts to keep him upright.

Keith turned around, glaring at the recruit. Realizing that he was going to get nowhere with him, Keith walked over to Anand and flipped him onto his back. He stared at Anand's helmet for a moment before starting to pull on it. Though he'd seen the advisors remove their helmets, Keith had never done it himself. Nonetheless, he found the removal tabs on either side and with a brief hiss, the helmet slid off. Upon the helmet's removal, Anand's head immediately fell back down to the ground. His dark face was caked with dried blood, his dark hair matted. His right eye was partially open, rolled back and dried out.

"Told ya." The recruit stepped up and kicked the side of Anand's body.

"Will you fuck off!" shouted Keith, his voice nearly cracking.

"Don't know about you, but I'm fucking done here. Once we get to wherever we're going, I'm out."

"Asshole."

Marco sighed, looking down at Anand's body. "Help me pick him up."

Keith looked up at Marco, nodded, and then started to pull Anand's left arm over his shoulder.

"Leave the helmet behind. It'll save on weight."

Keith nodded, dejected.

"Which way?"

Keith then gestured straight ahead with his chin. "This way. The woods are starting to look familiar."

"That's good."

As they started forward, Keith looked over at Marco. "How's your hand?"

"Not good." Marco held up his left hand. His middle finger was crooked, held on by a plethora of blood-stained bandages and tape.

Keith frowned.

They continued forward for another hour. They were pushing their way through a patch of thick bushes when woods lit up ahead. Keith signaled everyone to stop, then lowered Anand's body to the ground. Standing up straight again, he stared at the clearing up ahead for a minute before Marco spoke up.

86

"I think that's the old junk pile."

Keith nodded, squinting. "Yep, we're almost there."

Again, they picked up Anand before proceeding forward into the clearing. A pile of rusting metal and trash lay in the middle, with patches of sand and trampled dry grass all around. On the opposite side of the pile was a short dirt road. At the end of it, Keith could see farm fields. Echo Ranch.

Here, Keith and Marco instructed the other three recruits to wait. Echo Ranch was wary of anyone coming in from the North, more so of those emerging from the woods. The current situation between the Unified Dominion Armed Forces and the Earthers likely did not help. So, Marco and Keith would approach first and attempt to explain their situation and their guests. With any luck, the foreman (and hopefully the boss) would be in a good mood.

Before reaching the edge of the field, Keith and Marco stashed their rifles in a nearby briar patch. Neither Keith nor Marco trusted the other recruits enough to leave their arms with them, and it would be suicidal to approach Echo Ranch's sentries armed. As they stepped out into the field, they could see a laborer working the hay, maybe two hundred meters away. As soon as Keith and Marco were out of the shade of the trees, she spotted them. She froze for a moment before turning and shouting to a nearby sentry. At this, both Keith and Marco waved their arms wide. The sentry eyed them for a moment, his rifle partially raised, before turning and running away alongside the laborer.

"Ya'know, maybe we should have left the armor behind," said Marco.

"Fair point." Keith looked down at his flak jacket, then removed his helmet to wipe the sweat from his forehead. "What do you think we do now?"

"I'd say wait."

"You're right."

They stood in the sun for a few minutes, waiting. Soon enough, the dust cloud of an approaching vehicle could be seen. It was one of the ranch's trucks, this one with a large machinegun mounted on the back of the cab and eight men in the bed. As it stuttered to a stop, seven jumped out, weapons in hand, forming a skirmish line across the back edge of the field. Keith looked down at his boots uncomfortably. Though he'd been a part of the skirmish line before joining UDAF, he'd never been on the business end of it. After what felt like an eternity, one of the men began walking across the field towards them. As he reached the middle of the field, Keith recognized him as one of the foremen.

"Mani! Sollevato! Su!" the foreman shouted. It was rough Italian. Keith was never sure if the foreman actually spoke it or if he just made it up as he went.

Both Marco and Keith promptly raised their hands again, staring directly at the foreman as he approached. He was a big man, with dark skin and long black hair tied back under his faded khaki hat. Over his tattered blue shirt was a leather bandolier. It held a few magazines as well as a knotted string that supposedly represented how many northerners he'd killed. It wasn't until he was within twenty meters that he finally recognized Keith and Marco.

"The fuck!" he exclaimed loudly. "Where in the damned hells did you two come from?" he shouted as he closed the distance.

"We've been fighting Earthers, they-"

"Shut the hell up!" shouted the foreman, pointing at Keith with a thick finger. He then turned to Marco. "Your turn. Where the fuck are you two coming from?" He looked like he might explode.

"Gileppo Ranch, Mr. Sirko," answered Marco.

"You fighting with them or against them?"

Keith then spoked up again. "Neither, we-"

"I told you to shut up!" Sirko jammed his finger into the middle of Keith's vest before turning back to Marco. "So?"

"We weren't fighting them, but Gileppo's burned to the ground. Nothing left."

Sirko eyed Marco suspiciously for a few moments before speaking up again. "Is that so. Explains the number of guidos coming in looking for work. Fucks." He then turned to Keith. "Alright. Your turn. You done with your military parade?"

"No." Keith was now scowling. "My unit just came from Gileppo. We have injured, and we need water."

"Your unit." Sirko scoffed. "How many?"

"Four. Not including me and Marco."

"They back in the woods there?" Sirko looked over Keith's shoulder at the tree line.

"Yes."

"Go back there and bring them forward. Have them leave their weapons behind. Do you know where they're from?"

"No, I-"

"Doesn't matter. Either way, you'll be paying for whatever they use. 'Your unit,' probably ought to at least learn their names. Go. Go get them. Bring them here." As

Sirko said this, he waved back to the skirmish line, signaling them to move up.

Keith nodded, gritting his teeth. He'd probably seen more action in the last few weeks than Sirko had in his entire life, and here Sirko was, talking down to him. As Keith proceeded back towards the woods, Marco turned to follow him, only to be stopped by Sirko and told to wait. At this point Keith didn't care. He needed water. The other recruits needed water. Sirko could stuff it. At the very least, Keith was hoping for a warmer welcome.

After bringing the rest of his unit (and Anand's body) forward, they all climbed into the back of the truck. It was a short drive across a few kilometers of fields. Echo Ranch had established itself as one of the larger cattle and grain farms in the region. With Gileppo gone, Echo likely had become one of the largest. The outer fields were almost exclusively grain. It was the easiest resource to replace in the event of raiding, and far less valuable than the cattle stowed in the inner fields. As they entered the cow pastures, the farmhouses in the center of the property could be seen. The largest house was centrally located, serving both as the offices and living quarters for the boss and his family. Around it was a variety of smaller structures, ranging from blocky worker quarters and vehicle barns to industrial freezers for Echo Ranch's product. Nearly every building that wasn't a freezer was covered in faded-red paint.

All eyes were on them as they drove into the yard. Standing up in the back of the truck, Keith removed his helmet and waved to those he recognized. Most waved back, though looks of confusion and concern were prevalent. As they pulled to a stop in front of the main ranch house, Sirko ordered them all out. Keith and his recruits were immediately brought onto the covered porch on the front of the building and made to remove their flak jackets and helmets, which the ranch hands proceeded to search. Finally, a young lady came around with a tray and cups of water. She was one of the girls that Keith had courted before his departure to UDAF. As she walked by, he tried to strike up a conversation with her, but she awkwardly ignored him, walking away as soon as he'd taken a cup from the tray. Keith's heart sank. Not a warm welcome at all.

Keith finished his water quickly, then looked down at his burned and abraded arms. Looking up at one of the ranch hands, he asked, "When do you think we can hit the shower stalls? We had a run-in with some Sandjacks last night, and I'm burning like a motherfucker."

"All in good time," the ranch hand answered, eyeing the other recruits. He was leaning up against the wall, a rifle cradled in his arms. "You know where they're from?" he asked quietly, gesturing towards them.

"No." Keith frowned.

"Aight." The hand nodded. "Stand by for a few. The boss wants to talk to you."

"Shit," Keith mumbled. It was a rare occasion that a ranch hand (which Keith was) spoke to the boss, and it seldom turned out well.

Not a moment later, Sirko stepped out the front door and said, "Send him in."

The ranch hand held back a laugh before looking back at Keith. "Aight then."

Keith stood up, glancing at his recruits for a moment before stepping in. The hand walked a step behind Keith, still carrying his rifle. Keith looked at the floor uncomfortably as he walked. It felt like death row. Turning a corner, Keith suddenly found himself in the boss' office. There was a faded red and gold carpet on the floor. In the middle of the room was a large, dark-wood desk facing the door. The boss sat behind it. He was a big man, wearing a white pinstripe suit. His mustache and hair were as white as the suit and trimmed perfectly. As Keith looked around, he noticed one of the other foremen sitting in the back corner of the room, arms crossed.

"Sit down," said the boss, gesturing towards a chair.

The chair had a cloth cover over it. Sitting down, Keith immediately understood why, as the dirt and cuts on his arms immediately proceeded to stain it. "Mr. Ardavan," said Keith, unsure what to do.

"Keith Lane, correct?" asked Mr. Ardavan, turning side to side slowly in his chair.

"Yes sir, Mr. Ardavan."

"And prior to leaving, you helped tend the fields? Keeping the Razorcats away?"

"Yes sir."

"Alright then." Mr. Ardavan sat up straighter in his chair. "So, I understand you joined the 'Unified Dominion Armed Forces.' That's what they call themselves?"

"Yes sir. Sorry that I left on such short notice, I-"

"That's not what I'm worried about right now." Mr. Ardavan cut in. "So, Gileppo's been burned down. What happened?"

"Where should I start?"

"From the beginning. Why were you there?"

Keith swallowed. "UDAF has been fighting the Earther's. We've been doing a good job of it. The Earthers were attacking from the North, and UDAF had set up trenches in Gileppo's fields. They, the Earthers, attacked, and we tried to hold them off. They ended up destroying everything there."

"Were you fighting for or with Gileppo?"

"I'm not sure."

"And you're sure Gileppo Ranch is gone?"

"As far as I could tell. Everything was blown up or burnt down."

"Alright then." Mr. Ardavan exhaled. "UDAF. What's your role with them?"

"I was a recruit, but they promoted me. I have, or rather, had a unit. What's left is outside. Or rather, I was an assistant to one of the advisors who lead the unit." Keith was starting to stammer.

"And do you know where they're from? The Unified Dominion Armed Forces, where did they come from?"

"I think they're from off-world."

"Are you sure?"

"Pretty sure." Keith looked down at his feet.

There was a pause, then Mr. Ardavan spoke up again. "The Earther's stopped by here a few days ago."

"Wait, what?" Keith looked up at Mr. Ardavan. His expression was dead serious.

"A group of them came, a few vehicles, a bunch of men. They were asking about UDAF, what side we were on. Telling us not to worry."

Keith's stared at Ardavan, his mouth agape.

"I told them that we have nothing to do with UDAF. When they asked if any of our people were working with UDAF, I told them no."

"So, uh," Keith babbled, not sure what to say. "They didn't attack?"

"No, and if everything goes my way, we're not going to give them a reason to. Given what happened to Gileppo, I'm sure you understand why."

"Yes sir."

"Now, about you. Are you here to stay?" The boss' tone was unnervingly neutral.

"I signed a contract with UDAF. I really should return…" Keith again looked back down at the floor. He wasn't sure if the words out his mouth were the right ones or the wrong ones, and he certainly hadn't thought them through.

"Whatever you do," Mr. Ardavan leaned forward. "Do not associate this ranch with UDAF. If you get captured, if they start asking questions, you'd best make something up. Because if the Earthers bring you back here, I don't know you. The foremen don't know you either."

At this, the foreman sitting in the corner of the room nodded, his expression grim.

"And one last thing," Mr. Ardavan continued. "Your plot here."

Keith's heart sank. "What about it, sir?"

"A deal is a deal. That plot belonged to your father. It still belongs to you. But there is one thing *I* want. Should you make it back alive, I want to know everything you know about UDAF. Who they are, why they're here. It's a small thing to ask, and I expect you'll provide it."

"Yes, Mr. Ardavan." Keith nodded, not that he had much of a choice.

"Also, make sure to stop by within the year, show us you're still alive. A dead man's plot is useless land."

"Yes, Mr. Ardavan."

"Now, you and your boys may stay here the night. They'll be staying with you on your plot. See that they're gone by morning. Whether or not you go with them is your choice. You may leave."

"Yes, Mr. Ardavan, sir." Keith nodded, stood up, and left the office.

Chapter 12 – Home Again

'Should you make it back alive.' The boss' words reverberated in Keith's mind. Through all the bullets and explosions, the idea that he might end up in a ditch somewhere had never occurred to him. He lay in his bed atop the blankets, staring at the dimly lit ceiling. The thought disquieted him. Keith's house consisted of only one room, with a bed on one side and his dressers on the other. The rest of his stuff hung from beams that extended across the ceiling. Half of the items were practical implements; tools, utensils, and such. The other half was old technology that Keith had collected over the years. Near to none of the devices worked, but the smooth faces and complex materials they were made of had to mean that they were valuable. That, and Keith intended to fix them should the parts ever turn up. Not that he knew how to.

Taking a deep breath, he sat up, again pushing some dust off the side of the bed. He'd accidentally left a window open the day he left for UDAF. Since then, dust had been blowing in from the yard for the better part of two months. Upon getting back, he and most of his crew spent half the afternoon sweeping the place out. This was especially nice on Marco's part since he had his own home on Echo to go back to. Unfortunately, there was only so much that could be done. The sandy dust had permeated everything. The one member who didn't help, the same asshole who refused to help with Anand's body, Keith kicked off the property. Keith didn't really care about where the asshole went or what he did from this point on. That, and the other members of his crew didn't have any qualms about it, so Keith had no regrets. It was nice to be able to exact some form of revenge for once.

Earlier in the day, Marco had gone to the doctor to get his hand worked on. Keith hadn't seen him since. It was assumed that Marco was probably taking the time to visit with his family, so Keith wasn't worried. Keith and everyone else spent the time getting cleaned up and patched up. The ranch's showers were a welcome relief. Now, one recruit lay on a makeshift mattress on the floor opposite the bed. The other sat in a corner, his eyes closed.

Keith lay back down in his bed. "Hey, guys."

"Sup?" the recruit in the corner answered, his eyes still closed.

"I must apologize, I didn't quite get your names."

"Rudolph."

"Nice to meet you. And you?" Keith tilted his head slightly towards the recruit lying on the floor.

"Call me Ambrus."

"Where y'all from?"

100

Rudolph opened his eyes and yawned. "New Mantua."

"Never been up there. How is it?"

"Crowded."

When it became clear that Rudolph had nothing more to say, Ambrus spoke up. "Nomad. No specific territory."

Keith looked over at him. "I've heard about you guys."

"Not surprised. A lot of the local ranches get animals from our herds."

"Is it true that you guys figured out how to tame Razorcats?"

"No." Ambrus raised his eyebrows. "Where'd you hear that?"

"Gossip."

Their conversation was then interrupted by a knock on the door.

"One moment!" Keith said loudly, stretching as he again sat up. He was stiff from head to toe.

A moment later, he opened to the door to see Marco.

"How'd it turn out with the hand?" asked Keith.

Marco raised his left fist, which was now covered in clean bandages, a slight smirk on his face. "I'd flip you off if I could," he said, uncurling his fingers to reveal that the middle one was completely missing.

"Holy shit!" said Keith, wide-eyed.

"Aye, doctors numbed me up. Can't say I don't miss it."

"I…"

"Ain't your fault Keith," said Marco, slapping him on the shoulder. "Mind if I come in?"

"Not at all." Keith pulled out a second chair from the back, which Marco promptly sat in.

"Have you decided on UDAF?"

"I think I'll be going back. It seems like a good opportunity for me," answered Keith, sitting down on his bed. "You?"

"I think I'll go for one more run. One more paycheck like the last one, and I'll be set for a while."

102

"You're right there."

Rudolph then spoke up. "Fuckin' lost mine. Still in my tent at that camp."

"With any luck, it'll still be there," answered Keith.

Keith thought about Rudolph's statement for a moment. Something was nagging at him. Feeling his pockets, he confirmed again that he still had his pay and livestock bonds. His thought process was then interrupted by another knock at the door.

"Seems you're popular today," remarked Ambrus.

"Yeah, man." Keith stood up and again opened the door. He was surprised to see the girl from earlier.

"Sarah! How are you?"

"I'm fine." She looked nervous.

"Come on in, I-"

"I won't be here long."

Keith looked at her questioningly.

"I think we should break it off."

Keith now stared at her blankly.

After a long pause, Sarah spoke up again. "I didn't know where you had gone. Many of us did not think you'd make it back."

"But I'm back now, aren't I? And I will be back again."

"I'm with someone else now."

A wave of dismay swept over Keith. He stared at her for a minute, trying to figure out if this was some sort of joke. When it became clear that it wasn't, he spoke up again. "Alright."

"I need to go now."

"Yeah." Without another word, Keith shut the door. He then turned around, staring at the floor and wiping some sweat from his brow.

"That sucks man," commented Ambrus.

"Bitch," added Rudolph.

Keith then sat down on the side of his bed for the third time. The repetition was pissing him off.

"So," started Marco, awkwardly. "Where's your dad's rifle?"

"Fuck!" Keith slammed his fist down into his mattress. That was what he'd left behind. "Fucking camp."

"Shit." Marco sighed. "So, what's the plan for tomorrow."

"Get up early. Buy some supplies and a wheelbarrow. Retrieve our gear. Return to the UDAF camp." Keith spoke the words in monotone, his eyes shut. He'd rehearsed the words in his head but wasn't expecting to be this angry when he said them.

"So, we'll be walking?"

"I can't afford a truck, so yes."

After a long pause, Marco stood up. "Don't know if it'll make you feel better, but it was the boss that sent me to join UDAF, to find out where you'd gone."

"Best thing I've heard all day." Keith's tone remained painfully neutral.

"You get some sleep. I'll see y'all in the morning."

Chapter 13 – Static

Felman and Loesche lay prone in the edge of the wood line overlooking the airfield. It was a little after 1:00 am, the stars in the sky providing only the faintest of illumination. Both wore full ghillie suits over their thermal signature suppressing combat armor. Even in daylight, they'd be undetectable. It took them six hours of creeping through the woods to get here, using their night vision to cut through the near-complete darkness.

When they'd first arrived four hours earlier, at least a hundred militiamen roamed in and around the airfield. Among them were far more advanced troops, sporting modern combat armor and high-quality weapons. Now, only a few militiamen patrolled the edges of the airfield, with even fewer of the advanced troops supervising them. These were of interest to Felman and Loesche. It was clear that they were coordinating UDAF's militia, and that they were well trained. However, none sported any markings on their gear or weapons. More likely mercenaries if Felman had to bet on it.

Felman lowered his binoculars to better look over the entirety of the airfield. Like most things on Dominion, it was ill-maintained. Holes in the tarmac had been patched with compressed gravel, and near to none of runway edge lights worked. The "jet fighters" here were all re-fitted civilian aircraft, two-seaters with cannons bolted to the wings. Looking back down the slope, Felman watched as one of the mercenaries slowly paced back and forth along a rusted wire fence. He'd been considering trying to capture one of them, but the prospect was looking unrealistic. He brought his binoculars back up, setting them to record. The optics featured an integrated camera that transmitted a live feed back to the gunship. The more footage he could get of the mercs, the better.

Again, he focused in on the mercenary at the base of the hill, only to notice a red indicator in the corner of the display saying, "No Connection." He lowered the binoculars, attempting to wirelessly link the computer in his suit's gauntlet to the camera.

"Fuckin' piece of shit," he mumbled under his breath in Deutsch. He then turned on his comm line to Loesche. "Jaime, my camera's kaput. Yours running?" After a few moments of silence, he tried again. "Jaime?"

He then turned off his mask's voice suppressor and whispered to Loesche, "Jaime!"

"Why aren't you using comms?" Loesche whispered back.

"They aren't working."

"Lemme check… Shit, yeah."

"Give me a minute." Felman then attempted to open a channel with the gunship, but the rest of his equipment was showing 'no connection' as well. "Something's not right."

As he began to contemplate his options, he heard the faintest rustle in the woods to his right. Reaching left, he tapped Loesche on the shoulder and gestured in the direction of the sound. About 20 meters away, he could see two figures in black approaching slowly, rifles raised. A moment later, a third appeared farther to the right, this one with some sort of device strapped to his back.

Felman raised his sniper rifle, placing the crosshairs directly on the neck of one of the approaching figures. They were now within 15 meters, and he swore that he could hear the footsteps of a fourth. The line of men then stopped, the one with the backpack turning to whisper to another.

"'Iinahum qaribun."

Felman fired. The man he was aiming at immediately toppled to the ground clutching his throat. Meanwhile, the rest of the line erupted with fire and shouts.

"Alaitisal alsahih!"

Loesche then opened fire with his assault rifle, trying to shift as far back as he could through the thick low

108

growth. Felman took another shot, this time missing as his adversaries took cover.

Looking to the right at Loesche, Felman then said, "These are Novians! Let's get out of here!"

"Trying!" Sparks flew as a round scraped the top of Loesche's helmet, forcing him even lower to the ground.

Trying to backup, Felman fired another shot as a figure appeared a mere 10 meters away, forcing it down. Checking his comms, he again found himself stuck with the blinking message, "No Connection." Reaching down for his equipment belt, he began blindly searching for a grenade. He rarely needed one, so it was not conveniently stowed. He was then alerted by the sounds of gunfire echoing from the edge of the woods facing the airfield. Turning left, Felman observed as a militiaman blindly fired into the darkness, hitting somewhere between his position and the Novian's.

"We've really stirred up the hive now!"

"Fucking aye right!" answered Loesche, debris from shredded foliage raining down on him.

A flare was then launched from somewhere in the airfield, sending streaks of red light through the trees and wreaking havoc with his night vision. Peering left, Felman watched as another dozen militiamen advanced up the hill towards the tree line, firing wildly as they went.

"Loesche, stay down!"

Loesche responded with a thumbs up, then pressed his helmet into the dirt.

Within seconds the surrounding area became a veritable blender of fire as the UDAF militia advanced. Over the din, Felman could hear a few voices shouting, "cease fire!" in Spanish, though none the militia obliged. A shout of "tarajae!" could then be heard from the Novian side of the fight, at which point they proceeded to leapfrog back, covering each other as they went. Peering around as subtly as he could, Felman began charting a path back in the direction of the landing zone. Suddenly, a running militiaman tripped over Felman, falling to the ground next to him. Without a moment's thought, Felman's combat knife was out, slashing and stabbing him until he was unable to speak. With another few blows to the face, the militiaman's skull caved in, and he promptly stopped moving. Felman then crawled on top of the bleeding corpse, using his camouflage to hide it and him.

Within a few minutes, the firefight carried itself deeper into the brush towards the Novians. More UDAF militia followed it, entering the woods farther away from Felman and Loesche's position. Though the militiamen were still uncomfortably close, Felman decided to take the opportunity to get out of there. He signaled Loesche, and they began crawling away from the scene. Whatever was jamming the radio equipment was also making a mess of the integrated compass in Felman's gear, so they began the return trip blindly pushing through the low growth. It wasn't until they'd traversed nearly half a kilometer that their gear started working again, at which point Felman immediately began trying to re-establish a link with the gunship.

"Wasp to Starlight, do you read? Over."

After a few long moments, the gunship responded. "This is Starlight, we read you. We lost your signal earlier, what's your status? Over."

"Alert command, Novian Armed Forces are on the ground. We need immediate evac. Over."

"Received, passing along to command. Be advised; hostiles appear to be following-"

The radio transmission was then cut off, again replaced with static. Looking around, Felman couldn't see anything through the surrounding trees. He turned to Loesche.

"Turn off your comms. I think they're tracking us."

Loesche nodded, opening the panel on his left gauntlet and accessing his suit's settings. Felman did the same, again dismayed to find that his compass was awry.

"Let's go!" he whispered, and they proceeded forward at a jogging pace.

"Heads up, we've got critters to the left!" reported Loesche.

Looking left, Felman could see several tall, spindly figures among the trees. Each had to be at least two meters tall. As they continued running, what he thought were fallen trees up ahead began standing up and turning to face him. At the same time, the audio sensors in his helmet were filled with the sound of hissing.

"Cut right!" ordered Felman, as they turned to avoid the new arrivals.

They gave the creatures a wide berth, putting nearly twenty meters of distance between them. Fortunately, the critters did not seem eager to follow. By this point, Felman and Loesche were wheezing and choking on their own spit, the heavy gravity taking its toll. Cradling his sniper rifle in the crook of his left arm, Felman began accessing the screen in his left gauntlet again. Seeing that his onboard computer had a signal, he reactivated his comms and GPS.

"Wasp to Starlight, do you read?" he wheezed.

"Starlight here, go ahead."

"We're three-quarters of the way to the LZ. How's it looking behind us? Over."

"Hostiles are still in pursuit. Something seems to have slowed them down, over."

"Requesting a strafing run on hostiles in pursuit, over."

"Be advised; we do not know your exact position in relation to the target."

"Standby!" Felman looked over his shoulder to face Loesche. "Jaime, pull an IR strobe!"

"Got it!"

A few seconds later, when Loesche reported that he'd activated it, Felman got back on the radio.

"Wasp to Starlight, we've marked our position with a strobe. Fire free!"

"Fire free order received. Starlight inbound."

Almost immediately, a stream of white fire illuminated the sky, taking the tops off trees and raining material down onto Felman a Loesche. Two rockets followed, shaking the ground as they impacted.

"Jesus, that was close!" remarked Loesche.

A second stream of fire followed, sweeping the area behind them. The voice of the gunship pilot then came over the radio again. "Starlight to Wasp, be advised, targets are closing distance with you. We cannot continue to fire, over."

"Received," answered Felman. "Meet us at the LZ. We're coming in hot."

He turned to Loesche. "Get rid of that strobe!"

Without pause, Loesche threw the device as far as he could away from them.

"Wasp to Starlight, we're coming in from the east."

The roar of the gunship's engines could now be heard, white light from its electromagnetic thrusters illuminating the clearing ahead. Once they could see the gunship, Felman began waving his arms wide at the door gunner eyeing them. Suddenly the door gunner shouted, "stand clear!" while waving at Felman and Loesche to get down. Immediately, they both hit the dirt as the gunner opened fire into the woods behind them. "C'mon let's go!" Felman and Loesche got back up, staying as low as possible as they finished their run to the gunship. As soon as they climbed on board, the gunship took off and the door gunner retracted his machinegun, slamming the door shut behind them.

"Everyone, strap in!" shouted the flight crewman over the roar of the engines.

Felman and Loesche obliged, sitting down in the two available seats in the back of the craft. The rest of the seats were taken up by the door gunner and a squad of grunts, all of which now stared at Felman and Loesche.

"Are you OK, sir?" asked the squad medic, looking at Felman.

Felman's gear was covered in a mixture of spattered blood and sand. He looked down at his chest rig, pulling out an errant twig. "Yes, I am. It's been a busy night."

Chapter 14 – Detritus

It was nearly 10:00 am before they were leaving the ranch. Preparations to leave had drawn on for longer than anticipated, with bartering for supplies proving difficult. After having procured a cart, Keith and his crew pulled together over a day's supplies. It'd take at least that long to reach the UDAF camp on foot, and at least part of that trek would be over rough ground. Anand's body was loaded into the cart first, wrapped in a tarp and tied up. The body had thoroughly frozen overnight during its time in the industrial freezers. Combined with Anand's sealed combat armor, the smell wasn't too bad. Food and water were piled over him. Lastly, their armored vests, helmets, and weapons were returned to them – all intact. As harsh as the boss was, he was a man of his word.

As Keith performed a final check of the cart, he looked back at the main ranch house. Many among the ranch's population were present, watching the activity in the dusty courtyard. On the front deck stood multiple foremen, arms crossed and leaning back on the front wall. The boss stood with them, his hands in the pockets of his white suit. Like the foremen, his expression was troubled. Most everyone else appeared curious or concerned, more so the latter. Scanning the crowd once more, Keith confirmed that Sarah was not present. He exhaled through his nose, staring at the ground. Best not to think about it.

"We all set?" asked Marco, walking up with a backpack over his shoulder.

"As best we can be," answered Keith.

He looked over the surrounding buildings, taking in the faded-red paint of the houses and the stainless steel of the freezers. Time to go. Taking a deep breath, he grabbed one of the cart handles and lifted. Ambrus grabbed the other, and they proceeded onto the road, Rudolph and Marco on either side. As they left, not a word was spoken. No one, save Marco's family, even bothered to wave. It took about half an hour to reach the north edge of the property, at which point Keith and Marco ducked into the woods to retrieve their rifles from the briar patch they left them in the day before. From this point on, they picked up the pace as best they could.

A few hours in, they came upon the remains of a burnt-out truck in the middle of the road. It was still smoking, the burnt bodies of its occupants slumped forward in the cab or laid out in the road around it. Laying down the cart's handles, they approached the scene along the edges of the road, rifles in hand. As they got closer, it became clear that it was likely destroyed the day before, the remains having partially cooled. After confirming that there was no one else around, they walked up to the wreck.

"This thing looks like UDAF," commented Keith, looking at the burnt flak jackets scattered around the scene.

"Was UDAF," answered Rudolph, flipping over a corpse with his boot.

Coming around to the back of the truck, Keith observed multiple holes forming a dotted line across its bed. The holes continued through the body of the truck, with impacts in the ground where they'd passed clean through. Keith then looked up at the sky, where a shadow caught his eye.

"What's that?" he asked aloud.

The others then looked up as well. In the middle of the pale-yellow sky was a faint rectangular shape, silent and unmoving.

"I think that's a ship," answered Marco, squinting.

"We should hightail it out of here. I bet it's got guns," added Rudolph.

"They can hit us from up there?" Keith looked over at Rudolph.

"Us, and everything else." Rudolph began walking back to the cart at speed. "I'll help with the cart. Let's go."

Keith nodded and began walking back as well. Marco and Ambrus followed, only after picking ammunition off one of the burnt bodies. They again got underway, this time at a jogging pace despite the cart's weight. After half an hour of this, realizing that the looming specter of the ship overhead wasn't going anywhere, they slowed down to a walk. They couldn't hide from it and weren't going to outrun it, so tiring themselves out was pointless. Keith continued to glance up at it periodically, trying to make out any additional details. The vague yet immediate threat of it was both fascinating and terrifying to him.

Late afternoon they elected to stop, sore legs and empty stomachs being the primary motivators. That, and Keith's right calf muscles had begun to burn and cramp excessively, slowing down everyone. It'd started the night before but combined with the soreness of everything else he hadn't thought much of it. Now it was approaching unbearable. They pulled the cart off to the side and settled down in a dried-up drainage ditch along the road. After passing out supplies, they ate in silence. The heat of the day had tired them out, and quiet rest in the shade was far more appealing than any conversation that could be had.

By the time they got underway again, the sun was low in the trees, turning the sky a deep bronze. They continued forward in the twilight until they reached the junction in the road that led to the camp. Here they elected to stop for the night, practically blind in the darkness and too tired to pull the cart over the rough ground ahead. Keith volunteered for the first watch, sitting atop the cart and trying not to put pressure on his cramping right calf. By this point, he was starting to suspect an ailment, but he'd give it

119

until the next day to confirm. Not that he could do anything if he had contracted something.

The night passed quietly, so Keith and his crew were up and out at the crack of dawn. They reached the camp around mid-morning, being initially greeted by the sight of multiple derelict trucks. As they got closer, it became apparent that the camp had been quickly abandoned. The bodies they'd pulled out of the trucks three days earlier still lined the road. The advisor tents along the back of the field were gone, but the empty recruit tents remained. Multiple razorcats wandered slowly through the area, chewing on the corpses.

"So those are razorcats," remarked Rudolph, ignoring the rest of the scene.

"Don't get too close. They'll 'flick' you with those front legs," added Ambrus.

"Hurts?"

"Causes your guts to fall right out."

"Ah."

Razorcats were tall, spindly things, a little over two meters tall with four legs and white, chitinous exoskeletons. They had triangular heads atop long stiff necks, which they now craned low to reach the dead bodies on the ground. The tips of their front legs came to a sharp point and were serrated along the front like steak knives, granting them their nickname.

Keith stared at the scene, speechless. Finally, he spoke up. "You'd think that they'd at least bury the bodies!"

"You, my friend, have never served in a militia before, have you?" asked Ambrus.

Kieth turned to Ambrus, pissed.

"Such courtesies are not extended to us," he continued.

Keith turned away and shook his head. It didn't matter. "Maybe my father's rifle is still here."

He began limping his way into the field toward his tent. A few minutes later, he reached it, wincing as his right calf seized up again. Opening the front flap, he was relieved to find that his things were untouched. The rifle was still wrapped in his bedroll, his leather bandolier coiled up next to it. Grabbing both, he backed out and made his way towards the cart.

"Where to next?" asked Rudolph, looking over the field.

"Don't know. If there's anything else you want to grab, now's the time."

"Nothin' but shit here."

Keith placed his father's rifle in the cart then slung the bandolier across his chest. "You're right."

Again, they got underway, the summer sun beating down upon them. When they reached the main road, they elected to continue north. UDAF hadn't passed by Echo the night before, so it was the only direction they could have gone. Around mid-day, they stopped to rest in the shade. Due to the sun's strength and the consistently high temperatures on Dominion, it was customary to stop when the sun was highest. As Keith had learned from his time in the fields, trying to work these hours was typically fruitless. It was better to start earlier and work later when the sun wasn't at its peak.

Just as Keith was about to doze off, the rumble of a vehicle could be heard, jarring him awake. Down the road, a large dust cloud was visible. Keith and the others immediately reached for their weapons, readying themselves.

"Earthers!?" asked Keith, wide-eyed.

"I'm not sure," answered Ambrus, staring down the road. Meanwhile, Marco rushed deeper into the woods, positioning himself behind a tree.

While others ran for cover, Rudolph attempted to pull the cart deeper into the woods, only to tip it over. As

122

its contents spilled out into the dusty drainage ditch, he cursed, then ducked into cover with everyone else.

Suddenly, the vehicle came to a stop, kicking up dust around it. Seconds later, its rear doors swung open, depositing a squad of armed men.

"I think those are advisors," said Rudolph, squinting.

"Put your weapons down and come out!" shouted one of the men, his rifle still raised.

"Yep. Definitely advisors." Rudolph shrugged.

"Wait here," ordered Keith quietly, and he stepped out into the road. "We're trying to get back to camp. We have our advisor here…"

"Those guys in the brush, get them out here!" The advisors stopped ten meters away. In the background, Keith could see the turret of the APC turning towards them.

Keith looked at Ambrus, Marco, and Rudolph, waving at them to come out. Hesitantly, they put their weapons down and stepped into the road as well. With everyone now out in the open, five of the advisors came forward, their weapons lowered. The other five remained closer to the APC in a ready state, eyeing up the surrounding area.

"Where's your advisor?"

"In the cart."

The advisor walked over to the tipped over cart, pushing aside a bag of supplies to reveal Anand's body wrapped in plastic. "What happened to him?"

"Injured at Gileppo, didn't make it. We had to carry him back. We've been trying to regroup with UDAF since."

The advisor stared at Keith for a moment, his armored faceplate hiding any expression he might have had. "Alright. Grab what you can carry, hop in the APC. We'll be carrying your weapons."

Keith nodded, frustrated.

Keith, Marco, Ambrus, and Rudolph were able to grab nearly all the supplies minus the cart. Much to Keith's chagrin, the advisors would not permit him to tie the cart to the APC. It'd had been the most expensive part of this endeavor, and he was loath to leave it behind. As they made their way to the back of the APC, Keith's right calf completely seized up, forcing him to limp noticeably. The whole lower part of his leg felt like it was on fire. Within minutes they were all packed into the pack of the APC like sardines. Anand's body was tied to a stretcher that was laid out on their laps. Their supplies were piled on top of it, leaving barely any space in the cramped interior.

Once underway, Marco turned to Keith and asked, "You alright?"

"My leg's fucked." Keith winced as his muscles seized up again. "I think I've gotten gray-burn."

'Gray-burn' was an ailment unique to Dominion, resulting from a parasite that entered the body through abrasions in the skin. Once in, it caused muscles in the local area to secrete lactic acid excessively, causing them to cramp and burn. In the worst cases, oxygen to the affected area would be cut off, resulting in grey streaks and potentially necrosis. In the meantime, Keith would be dealing with red, inflamed skin, and constant cramps. He'd likely contracted it during the run through the woods two nights before. It'd take over a week to resolve itself – if it resolved itself. For now, Keith was best off trying not to move that leg, which was rapidly proving not to be an option.

Marco looked down at Keith's leg. "Shit, man. Wish I could help you."

Chapter 15 – Regroup

Keith squinted as he stepped out of the APC's dark interior. As his eyes adjusted to the bright sunlight, he began to look around at the surrounding buildings. Before he could get his bearings, however, an advisor pushed him from behind and told him to move. Unable to put any weight on his right leg, Keith promptly collapsed onto the dusty gravel.

"Fuck you, asshole! Fuck you!" shouted Keith, flipping over. The advisor stared back at him, emotionless through the armored faceplate.

Marco then stepped forward and helped Keith up.

"Go to that building over there. You will be debriefed," ordered the advisor.

Keith nodded, scowling. Marco then helped him down the road, Ambrus and Rudolph close behind. Four advisors flanked them, keeping them walking at a fast pace despite Keith's leg.

Unlike the camp, most of the advisors here appeared to be operating out of permanent buildings. Tarps were stretched out between them, providing cover for equipment and field kitchens. Numerous recruits roamed around the area, accompanied by better-armed troops that didn't appear to be advisors.

Recognizing them, Rudolph suddenly shouted, "Mantova prima! Mantova ultima!"

"Lunga vita alla nostra gente!" one of the troops shouted back, waving.

One of the escorting advisors then elbowed Rudolph, telling him to quiet down.

"What was that?" asked Keith, looking over his shoulder at Rudolph.

"New Mantuan army, my people!" It was the first time Keith had seen Rudolph happy.

Keith stared at the Mantuan troops marching by. Their armor mirrored that of the Earthers, featuring similar helmets and shoulder plates. Unlike the Earthers, the armor was painted dark yellow to match Dominion's sands.

Keith, Marco, and Rudolph were then asked to sit down on a bench outside of one of the buildings while Ambrus was brought in. Marco helped lower Keith down onto the bench before sitting down himself. Rudolph elected to stand, only to be ordered to sit down. The next twenty minutes were spent waiting, the four advisors staring down at them coldly. Finally, Ambrus was brought out, and Rudolph was ordered in. Rather than sitting down with Keith and Marco, Ambrus was walked away down the line of buildings out of sight. Another twenty minutes passed, during which Keith glared at the advisor who'd pushed him down. The advisor stared back, unmoving. Marco was the next to be brought in, leaving Keith alone on the bench.

Looking up at the advisors again, Keith asked sarcastically, "You expect me to walk up those stairs myself?"

"Our orders are to see that you make it in. You'll be carried if need be."

Keith then pointed at the advisor that pushed him down earlier. "He's an asshole, by the way."

None of the advisors responded.

Finally, Marco was walked out, and it was Keith's turn. One of the advisors stepped forward, lifting Keith up on his left side. Keith complied, and soon they were inside the building. Like the advisor tents at the camp, the interior of this place was frigid, so much so that Keith's sweat steamed off his hot skin. The advisor lowered Keith into an olive drab canvas chair in front of a large metal desk. Behind it sat Captain Kowal, who surprisingly looked to be in a good mood. Keith stared at him, unnerved by this and the captain's pink eyes.

"Welcome back. Mr. Lane, correct?"

128

"Yes." Keith watched as another man in a black uniform approached from the back of the room and leaned against a wall, watching them.

"I must apologize for the behavior of my men. They've been told to take every precaution against Earth Union spies."

"Huh." Keith stared back, unconvinced.

"I understand you spent your own money for the supplies to get you here?"

"Yes."

"You will be compensated in full, plus a bonus."

Keith's expression changed from one of open suspicion to confusion.

"We appreciate initiative. You showed it, and we believe that should be rewarded."

"Right." Keith took a deep breath. "Gileppo Ranch, what happened with that?"

"The Earth Union moved faster than we anticipated. Regarding your advisor, Anand. Could you tell me what happened to him?"

"He was shot at some point during the fighting. We carried him back to..." Keith trailed off.

"Back to where?"

"Echo Ranch. My home. He died before we could do anything for him, so we kept his body in a freezer for the overnight."

"Explains the freezer burns." Kowal leaned back in his chair. "The others told me that you were the one who brought them back here to rejoin our forces. Is this correct?"

"Yes. Your men brought us most of the way in their APC, though."

"Of course." Kowal chuckled. "I like that you had the wherewithal to execute all this. Not only did you stick with your group and carry them through that fight, but you returned. There are many still missing from that day. Should you choose to accept it, we would like to promote you. You've demonstrated a level of duty beyond what was expected of you, and we believe that you can be of great assistance to us." Kowal stopped for a moment, eyeing Keith. "Is something troubling you, Mr. Lane?"

Keith was silent for a moment before answering. "The camp. Everyone was where we left them. None of the bodies were buried."

"Ah," Kowal sighed. "We had to abandon the camp quickly. The Earthers could have arrived any minute."

"But they didn't."

"You saw the drone they sent. They knew we were there."

Keith frowned as he realized the reality of the situation, and how far-reaching Earth's capabilities were. The drones, the rockets, the starships. It all seemed impossible, until now.

"Mr. Lane."

"Yessir." Keith snapped to attention.

"Will you take the promotion?"

"Yes, yes sir. But I have one more question."

"Yes?" Kowal raised an eyebrow.

"Where are my men?"

"Mess tent, enjoying some well-earned desserts. Once the medic's looked over your leg, you'll be joining them."

Keith nodded, relieved.

A half-hour later, Keith exited the medical tent with a set of crutches. As Kowal had said, the medical staff looked him over and began a regimen of localized antibiotics to kill the parasites burning up his leg.

According to them, Keith would recover almost fully within a week. This was hard to believe, as Keith had never seen a case of grey-burn resolve in under a month. With any luck, though, the medical staff would be right. From here, he was directed to the mess tent, where one of the advisors held the flap open for him as he hopped his way in.

The interior was cooler than outside. Not frigid like the advisor quarters, but comfortable. Marco, Rudolph, and Ambrus sat at a table in the middle, already drunk and laughing. The rest of the mess tent was empty. Seeing that it was mid-afternoon and between meals, this made sense, though any special treatment tended to make Keith uncomfortable. He sat down as gently as he could, wincing as his leg proceeded to seize. It then cramped again as Rudolph slapped him on the back, laughing.

"Hey man, you got us here! We're in good shape now!"

A cook then came out of the back of the mess tent carrying a tray laden with mugs and bowls. As expected, the mugs were filled with beer. Much to Keith's surprise, each bowl was packed with ice cream. He stared at each, puppy-eyed as the cook laid them out. Back at Echo, they only had ice cream when there was a surplus of dairy, and it'd been a long time since that was the case.

"Yeah, we are!" answered Keith, picking up a spoon.

"Not just that," Ambrus cut in. "We've been fuckin' promoted! All of us!"

"Holy crap! Really?"

"Group leaders, man!" Ambrus slurred his speech as he said the words excitedly.

An hour and a lot of beer later, other recruits began filing in. By now, Keith was too drunk to feel his legs, and his head lolled as he watched the scene around him. As the other recruits began to line up for dinner, the cook came out one more time, now with a tray of regular rations and mugs filled with water.

"This ain't beer, man," slurred Keith, picking up one of the mugs.

"Drink it. You'll feel better tomorrow."

"Ok, man," answered Keith, looking back down at the mug cross-eyed then drinking from it.

A few minutes later, as he began to dig into his dinner, a familiar figure sat down across the table from him. "So, what's happened to you?"

Keith looked up at Gaz, surprised. "Holy fuck, man, you're alive! Holy shit."

"So are you."

"Barely," muttered Keith, trying to focus. "Hey, I've been promoted! Fuckin' aye."

Gaz looked at Keith hard. "What do they have you doing?"

"Don't know yet, but it's going to be fuckin' great!"

"He got us promoted too!" interjected Rudolph, looking up from his tray for the first time. "Group leaders!"

"Mhmm." Gaz looked back at Keith. "Keith, I need to tell you something. Keith?"

Keith looked up from his tray again, bleary-eyed.

"Perhaps now's not a good time."

"Shit, sorry man, I didn't…"

"No, no, no, you're good! Congratulations, man!" Gaz assured, though, by this point, it was questionable how much Keith was registering.

Chapter 16 – Stand Tall

Since his promotion, Keith had been assigned to a new advisor. Unlike Anand, this one was far more enthusiastic about having an assistant and included Keith in nearly all matters. In terms of his actual job, Keith oversaw three groups totaling thirty men, led by Marco, Rudolph, and Ambrus, respectively. Keith primarily handled the logistics side, assuring that gear, weapons, and ammunition was dispensed as needed, and that said items did not disappear mysteriously. Command in combat was primarily handled by Keith's new advisor, Wilson, though he typically made sure that Keith was learning as much as possible in this regard. Furthermore, Wilson had procured new gear for Keith. Minus the helmet, he looked like one of the advisors.

"Good morning, Advisor Wilson!" said Keith, hopping down from the cab of his truck and standing as straight as he could.

"Good morning, Keith. How's the leg?"

"Still stiff, sir."

"You're steadier than last week, progress!"

"Thank you, sir!"

"Here are the assignments for today," said Wilson, handing Keith a map. "GPS already has the coordinates programmed in. Just follow the column, and you'll be good to go."

"Combat?"

"Just peacekeeping today. Something's riled up our neighbors."

"Got it."

Since the destruction of Gileppo Ranch, it'd become readily apparent to the other territories that the rumors of Earthers on-world were true. This led to a large influx of new recruits, so much so that procuring enough weapons for them was proving difficult. Fortunately for UDAF, since the New Mantuan army had gotten involved, they had more time to focus on logistics and outreach to further territories. Thus far, with few exceptions, UDAF had been very successful.

Climbing back into the cab of the truck, Keith unfolded the map and looked it over. Today they'd be going to Forsythe Ranch, farther east and closer to the shoreline. Another advisor, Advisor Byrne, then hopped into the passenger seat.

"Top of the morning to you," he said, leaning over to look at the map. "Couldn't be an easy one today, could it?"

136

"We'll get there." Keith traced his finger along one of the winding roads leading towards Forsythe. There didn't seem to be a single direct route.

The truck bounced slightly as Ambrus and his group hopped into the back. Turning to look through the back window, Keith waited for the thumbs up from Ambrus before starting the truck and rolling forward. As they got underway, Byrne climbed up onto the gunner's step and took control of the heavy machinegun above the cab. Thankfully, up to now, they hadn't needed it.

Three hours later, they rolled into an industrial yard belonging to Forsythe. The ranchers eyed them with suspicion as the trucks pulled in, weapons in hand. In addition to that, something didn't sit right with Keith. Looking around, he started to notice the number of bullet holes that pockmarked the surrounding buildings. Next to one of the prefab offices, Keith realized that what he thought was an oil stain was blood spatter. He stared at the angry men standing around the yard as he slowed the truck to a stop - never had he felt so exposed.

"All units, standby," ordered Wilson over the radio.

Keith watched as Wilson exited the second truck in the column, one advisor with him, and approached what appeared to be one of Forsythe's foremen. The foreman immediately broke into a tangent, shouting at Wilson and pointing at the column. Wilson tried to calm the foreman down to no avail. Meanwhile, the other advisor surveyed the area, keeping an eye on the angry ranchers surrounding them. Finally, the foreman's tangent was over, and Wilson began walking back to the column, visibly pissed.

"Any idea what's up?" asked Keith, looking up at Byrne in the gunner's position.

"We'll know soon enough." He sounded concerned.

A few minutes later, Advisor Wilson came in over the radio. "All units, be advised: One of our platoons has gone rogue. We've been greenlit to terminate. Advise your groups. Standby."

"Does that mean what I think it means?" asked Keith in disbelief.

"Yup. Stay on the wheel. I'll update everyone." Byrne then turned around to face the bed of the truck and began relaying the information to Ambrus.

Keith nodded. Unsure what to do, he began checking all of the lights on his truck's dashboard, trying to stave off a feeling of dread in the pit of his stomach. Within minutes, new coordinates came in. Though the advisors had been teaching Keith how to read, he was still far from proficient at it. Nonetheless, after a few minutes, he managed to get the coordinates entered just as the column started to move forward.

"Alright, let's go!" said Byrne, tapping the roof the cab twice.

The truck shuttered forward, and they were underway, this time much faster.

"Byrne?"

"Yeah?" He looked down at Keith.

"I hate to say it, but how good are fixed coordinates? Wouldn't they be moving?"

"I'm sure Mr. Wilson has thought of that. They've probably locked on to the transponder of the platoon advisor."

"Would one of you guys seriously go rogue?"

"That's what concerns me. I don't think so."

An hour later, they got their answer. Slowing to a stop, Keith could see a truck pulled off to the side of the road, multiple bodies on the ground around it. Ambrus and his group then piled out, creating a perimeter around Keith's truck. Byrne remained in the gunner's position, swinging the gun around to scan the woods on either side. Up ahead, Marco's group secured the area around the truck, checking the bodies. Flipping over one of the corpses, Marco then called over Advisor Wilson, who immediately ran over.

"Looks like they found the advisor," remarked Byrne, watching the scene unfold. "Fuck, I know that guy."

The advisor had been shot through the head and was mostly stripped of his equipment and clothing. The other bodies were the same, appearing to have been killed execution-style or shot in the back trying to escape. Nearly all of them had been mutilated to some extent. Keith stared at the scene, mouth agape. His trance was then interrupted by Wilson's angry voice over the radio.

"New coordinates sent. We're oscar mike."

"Everybody mount up!" shouted Byrne to Ambrus's group, who quickly obliged.

Once underway, Wilson came over the radio again. "We believe we've located the position of the two stolen trucks. Engage on sight. Copy?"

"Received," answered Byrne through his helmet's integrated radio. He then turned and relayed the information to Ambrus in the back. Once he'd done this, he lowered himself back into the cab and turned to Keith. "When we get there, stop the truck, engage the E-brake, and get out. Stay with the truck, though. You got me?"

"Yessir." Keith nodded quickly, white-knuckling the steering wheel.

"Keith, this isn't your first rodeo. It's messy business, but you'll do fine."

"Yup."

Byrne then climbed back up into the gunner's position, turning to Ambrus. "When we get there, swing your guys right. Got it?"

"Yes sir!" answered Ambrus.

It wasn't long before they came upon the deserters. As the column began to turn right around a bend, the lead truck suddenly came to a stop, and shouts could be heard. As Keith slammed on the brakes, the pops of gunfire rang out ahead, though the source was obscured by a rocky outcrop along the interior of the bend.

Turning to Ambrus, Byrne shouted, "Take your guys and secure that hill!" He pointed at the outcrop.

Not a moment later, the ping of a rifle round ricocheting off the top of the cab could be heard. Keith slammed the E-brake down with his foot, swung open the door, and practically rolled out onto the sandy road. Ambrus's group did the same, half piling out the back while the others bailed out over the side opposite the outcrop. Collecting himself, Keith reached back up into the cab and grabbed his rifle, flipping the safety off and bringing it up to his shoulder. Ambrus and his guys were already returning fire. Keith then swung around the front of the truck and put two rounds into the chest of a man barely ten meters away. Ducking back, he looked into the cab and was surprised to see Byrne still in the gunner's position.

"Byrne? Byrne!" He reached into the cab and began pulling Byrne down.

Getting Byrne down onto the driver's seat, Keith pulled again, nearly dropping him onto the ground. Upon seeing the amount of blood, both on him and the sand, Keith grabbed a medical kit from behind the driver's seat. Attempting to rip it open, he found himself unable to as his bloody hands slipped along the sealed plastic packaging.

"Somebody fucking help me!" Keith shouted, now shaking.

Almost immediately, Ambrus was by his side. "Where you hit?"

"No, no! Him!" Keith shoved the medical kit into Ambrus's hands and began trying to apply pressure to the wound beneath Byrne's armpit. "Byrne! Are you with me?"

"Fucking aye, they got me good," groaned Byrne, blood pouring out of his side.

"Where are those fucking bandages!?"

"Slow down, Keith! We need to get the armor off!" shouted Ambrus.

142

They undid the Velcro and straps holding the armor on as quickly as they could, only to be greeted by more blood spurting out. Unable to locate the hole, they began packing bandages over Byrne's entire left side.

"Byrne! You still with me?" Keith began pulling at the tabs on the sides of Byrne's helmet, releasing them then pulling it off. "Byrne?" Byrne's wide face was pale, his eyes half-closed. Momentarily putting his left hand over Byrne's mouth, Keith confirmed that he was still breathing. He keyed his radio. "We have an advisor down! Truck 3!" He looked back down at Byrne. "Come on, man! No, no!"

Keith began pounding on Byrne's chest, but Ambrus stopped him. Looking up at Ambrus, Keith realized that sounds of gunfire had stopped. He looked back down at Byrne.

"What, no." Keith leaned forward over Byrne's dead body. Before anything more could be said, Wilson and another advisor had arrived, medical bags in hand.

"Where's he hit?" asked the advisor.

When Keith found himself unable to speak, Ambrus answered. "Left side. Armpit, I think."

Wilson and the other advisor immediately got to work. Ambrus then grabbed Keith and pulled him away. Walking to the next truck in the column, the scene of the main firefight came into view. The two trucks belonging to the traitors were stopped in the middle of the road, bodies in and around them. Both had their hoods open, with a variety of parts spread out over the ground in front of them. The few traitors that survived the engagement were now being lined up alongside the rear truck. When all of them were accounted for, an advisor stepped up and executed the remainder with his rifle. Without pause, he then shouted, "Gather their arms and mount up! We're done here."

Chapter 17 – Reinforcements

"Where's that air cover? We need it now!"

The ground vibrated as the platoon of New Mantuan tanks rolled inexorably across the field. Among them, New Mantuan regulars advanced on foot in skirmish lines, firing as they went. The attack had started unexpectedly that morning with an artillery bombardment, and now the ground forces had arrived to mop up the Earth Union conscripts in their trenches.

Loesche keyed his mic again. "Wasp to command! Hostiles are less than a click away, relaying new coordinates."

Felman peered up over the edge of the trench with his range finder. "600 meters!"

A shot from one of the tanks then slammed the ground thirty meters in front of Felman, spraying him with dirt and debris.

"Thank god, they suck at aiming!" shouted a conscript down the line. His squad leader promptly told him to shut up.

Like everything in this campaign, logistics were badly planned. For every hundred rifles, there was maybe a single light anti-tank weapon. Better suited for taking out trucks and light armor than main battle tanks – even outdated ones. Felman watched as a missile from one hit a tank point-blank and proceeded to bounce. Cheaply made things.

"God-rod incoming! Everybody get down!" shouted Loesche, signaling wide with both his hands.

Realizing what this meant, Felman immediately got as close to the trench floor as he could. Taking the hint, the conscripts began taking cover. The air itself then split.

For a moment, there was a bright flash. Then the ground seemed to lift. A blast wave followed, sending a hail of rocks and splintered trees flying over the top of the trench. The wind direction then reversed, pulling back towards the source of the blast. As it subsided, Felman got back up on his feet, brushing dust off his armor. What used to be the field was now a massive cloud of debris, raining down over the surrounding area. A hundred or so meters away, a tank turret slammed into the ground, half burying itself sideways.

"Way too close," remarked Felman.

"Yeah, way too close," Loesche agreed.

An hour later, they arrived back at the airfield, now under Earth Union control. Since their reconnaissance mission three weeks earlier, Central had finally granted the ground forces permission to take priority targets by force, though stringent rules of engagement remained. However, the single combat division was rapidly proving insufficient to hold any substantial ground. Furthermore, since the city of New Mantua had mobilized against them, the Earth Union expeditionary force had been unable to do much more than protect territory already under its control. If it weren't for the sudden authorization to use orbital weapons, Earth Union forces likely would have been overrun.

Walking up to the prefabricated headquarters building, Felman and Loesche removed their helmets. Turning his helmet on its side, Felman remarked, "Going to need a new set of hearing sensors."

Loesche cursed in Deutsch, looking over his helmet and removing one of the hearing modules. Its diaphragm was clearly blown out, exposing the dust-coated electronics underneath. By now, they had reached the front entrance of the command post, which a guard opened without question. Felman and Loesche had become celebrities of sorts, supermen among the hordes of conscripts. It made Felman uncomfortable. Composing themselves, they stepped in, their helmets under their arms.

"Good afternoon sir-" Felman stuttered as he was surprised by a man in a suit and tie rather than Captain Healy.

"Good afternoon, Sergeant. I've heard a lot about you." The man extended his hand.

Felman shook it, then the man turned to Loesche, shaking his hand. "Specialist Loesche, I hear that there isn't a better spotter to be found!"

"Thank you… sir." Loesche looked as confused as Felman.

"Bennett Couture, it's good to meet you two."

Felman looked over Couture. His suit was black with grey pinstripes and neatly pressed, far too nice for military intelligence. On his wrist was a gold-plated Sovereign Brand watch, a wildly expensive piece. "I must apologize, sir. I do not know your rank."

"No rank, Sergeant. I'm from Central, Board of Military Affairs." Couture smiled.

"Where is Captain Healy?"

"He's been replaced." Couture coughed. "It was decided that someone more invested in Earth's mission here was needed."

Felman stared at Couture for a moment. "So, you're in charge?"

"Yes, I am." Couture smiled. "And now that I'm here, I believe that Central will be more open to getting things done. I've authorized the use of our orbital arsenal as I'm sure you've noticed."

"It was hard not to, sir."

Couture chuckled. "Anyhow, if you could please provide me with an update on your investigation. I've read the reports, but I'd like to hear it from you." He leaned back against what used to be Captain Healy's desk.

"Where would you like me to start?"

"The mercenaries, if you please."

"Yes sir." Felman collected thoughts before proceeding. "The mercenaries are from off-world. Though we have yet to capture any alive, their physiology is not in line with lifelong Dominion natives. You'd have to talk to the coroner for specifics, but their bloodwork indicates that at least some of them are from Novus."

"Do you believe that they are Novian military?"

"We do not believe so at this time, though they appear to be coordinating with Novian special forces, which would explain some of the anomalies we've had with our equipment. Currently, we believe there to be at least one Novian electronic warfare unit on world, if not more."

Couture nodded. "I've already put in a request for elements of the 81st Electronic Warfare Brigade. With any luck, they'll put an end to the jamming."

Felman raised his eyebrows. "I thought they were finishing up operations on Echelon?"

"*Finished* up operations. Officially they are still there, though. Best if you didn't spread that one around."

"Certainly, sir."

"New Mantua was experiencing some of these anomalies as well, yes?"

"Yes sir. When we initially landed, the locals were blaming us for their communications blackouts. We've since concluded that this was a Novian strategy to turn the local population against us."

"And indeed, they did." Couture took a deep breath. "With New Mantua aligned against us, a peaceful takeover is no longer on the table."

"With all due respect, sir, we do not have enough equipment and personnel on world to continue this campaign."

"We at Central prefer the term 'reintegration.' Rest assured, Sergeant. I've made arrangements for reinforcements. This operation will be concluded in a month." Couture stood back up. "In the meantime, is there anything you're in need of?"

To this, Felman lifted his helmet slightly. "New hearing modules, sir."

"I'll see that you get them."

A half-hour later, Felman and Loesche stepped out of the headquarters building into the Dominion sun. Squinting up at the pale-yellow sky, Felman rummaged through one of his pouches before pulling out a dusty, olive green cap and putting it on. "I didn't think we were winning on Echelon."

"I don't think we did," answered Loesche.

"I think you're right." Felman pulled down the brim of his cap to better shield his eyes from the sun.

Proceeding to the mess tent, Felman and Loesche sat down with the squad that Captain Healy had assigned to them. Healy's judgment had been sound. Though this squad was green, they were competent and had proven helpful in pulling Felman and Loesche out of some sticky situations. As they sat down, one of the privates stood up and said, "Good afternoon to the ober men!"

"That's 'Übermenschen' to you," answered Felman, to which the squad laughed.

"Hey bruv," another private elbowed Loesche. "You hear the news? African Union's sending a whole fuckin' combat division."

"Where on Earth did you hear that?" asked Loesche, incredulous.

"Not on Earth no more. I was talkin' to one of the Seabees. They say the Africans will be here any day now!"

Another one of the infantrymen then cut in, "Couldn't be bothered to join the Earth Union, and now they're reaping the benefits of our expansion!"

"I suppose it's fitting. The Doms don't have gene standards. The African Union doesn't enforce them. They'll get along just fine!"

Felman watched as the dialog degenerated into ripping on the various African states, confused. Decades earlier, when the Earth Union was formed, it was composed primarily of the Americas, Europe, and Asia. Having chosen not to align with Earth Union domestic and economic policies, the dominant African states had elected to form their own alliance. The African Union, as it came to be called, eventually encompassed the near entirety of the African continent, all the way up into parts of the Middle East. It'd since built the most powerful economy in human-controlled space, dramatically outpacing the Earth Union and even Novus. The African Union's only setback was its lack of reach into space, primarily the result of

152

aggressive sanctions by the Earth Union Central Government. Seeing that barely five years earlier, the Earth Union had been on the brink of war with the African Union, their arrival on Dominion as allies seemed unlikely.

Just as Felman opened his mouth to start asking questions, the roar of dropship thrusters could be heard overhead. Peering out the side of the mess tent, his jaw dropped as a massive tan dropship lowered itself onto the landing strip. "No fucking way," Felman mumbled in Mars-Deutsch, standing up from the table and walking towards the edge of the tarmac.

Painted across the front of the cockpit was the yellow snarling maw of a lion, Swahili and Amharic phrases scrawled around it. The assault doors on the back of the drop ship then slammed down, and a platoon of Sudanese infantry piled out, waving their fists in the air and shouting in broken English at the Earth Union personnel scattered about the airfield.

"Even the mighty Earth Union needs our help now!" shouted one of the soldiers, slapping the top of his helmet and laughing at Felman.

Their commander then shouted, "Order!" at which point troops lined up and quieted down. "Machi!" They then began marching down the airfield. Meanwhile, another half dozen dropships appeared on the horizon. Felman stared at the scene uncomprehendingly.

"So, these are Couture's reinforcements?" asked Loesche.

Felman jumped, having not heard Loesche's approach. "I supposed so..." He watched as another drop ship hovered close to the ground, depositing a tan and brown main battle tank.

"Well, now we've got the manpower."

"That we do."

Chapter 18 – Contraction

Keith awoke with a start. Looking up, he was surprised to see Advisor Byrne, standing over him. He blinked, and Byrne was gone. The low rumble of a distant explosion then brought him to his senses.

"Fuck..." he mumbled, rubbing his eyes and throwing his blankets aside.

Swinging his legs over the side of his bed, he stood up and immediately began pulling his coverall on, followed by his armored vest and helmet. Within moments he was fully kitted, at which point he flipped on his radio and picked up his rifle.

"Advisor Wilson, what's going on?" he asked over the radio as he exited his room.

Stepping out into the hot morning sun, more rumbles could be heard, followed by the roar of aircraft engines.

"All sections, ready yourselves!" he shouted at the top of his lungs towards his platoon's group of tents. He was relieved to see that they were already scrambling out, weapons in hand. Rudolph and his group were the first to get to Keith, standing at attention.

"Keith, what's going on?"

"Not sure yet." Keith rubbed his eyes again, the creeping feeling of a fatigue-driven headache looming over him. He then keyed his mic. "Advisor Wilson, Group 2 is ready!" A few minutes later, Ambrus and Marco arrived, followed by their men. All eyes were on Keith now. Keith keyed his mic again, "Advisor Wilson, platoon is-"He was cut off by a sudden, familiar, unnerving buzz. "Everybody get down!" Keith's voice cracked as he shouted the words.

As the platoon hit the dirt or scrambled for cover, a white beam of fire zipped along the road, mulching those unlucky enough to be caught in its path. Not a second later, the headquarters building exploded, sending burning debris flying across the sandy street.

Pulling up the brim of his helmet, Keith looked over his men. Nearly everyone was OK. Two red smears marked the last positions of those who were not. "Everyone regroup! South side! Now!" he shouted as clearly as he could, picking up his rifle and scrambling to his feet. Turning left, he began running along the canvas wall that composed the mess tent. Around him, recruits from other groups ran in all directions, some firing erratically into the air towards the source of the buzzing.

Reaching the base's south edge, he vaulted over a concrete barricade and took cover behind it. The three groups that composed his platoon followed, Rudolph in the

156

lead. As men piled in behind the limited cover, Keith started taking count. At least another two guys were now unaccounted for. Peering around the barricade, he spotted one of his recruits taking cover behind the corner of a nearby building. Only one unaccounted for. In the background, he spotted the source of the beams, a black dot just above the horizon. Another buzz followed, a shot striking the edge of the barricade just as he pulled back behind it.

"OK, guys," he took a deep breath. "Spread out, stick with your team leaders! Marco, you're with me!"

At this, Ambrus took his guys left, sprinting to the nearest building. Rudolph and his group followed, narrowly dodging one of the beams. Marco and his group remained packed behind the two concrete barricades with Keith. Before Keith could decide where to go, Wilson came in over the radio.

"Keith, get to the command post ASAP!"

"Sir, command post is destroyed!"

"Get over here now!"

Keith nodded to himself. "Yessir!" He then turned to Marco and his group. "Alright let's go!"

Electing to avoid the main road, they began their run around the base's outside edge to the command post.

Soon enough, Keith had reached it, and was surprised by the number of advisors climbing through the rubble. Among them was a young woman in a tattered business suit, an assault rifle slung over her shoulder, trying to pull a body to cover.

"Keith, help me out!"

Wilson was difficult to pick out among all the armored advisors, so Keith ran towards the source of the voice. Within moments he was helping to pull rubble off another body. Moving aside a piece of sheet metal, Keith's heart dropped as he looked upon the broken body of a woman, the attractive blonde he'd seen at the camp north of Echo two months before.

"Let's get her up."

Keith snapped out of it, and soon she was free. If she was alive, Keith couldn't tell, not that he had time to check. The scream of missiles overhead and that unnerving buzz had returned, forcing Keith as low to the ground as he could get. The advisors followed, running for cover every which way.

"This is fucked!" shouted Keith.

"Just hold on a minute!" Wilson shouted back. He had his left hand up to his helmet's earpiece, trying to adjust his integrated radio.

Another missile shot overhead, this time in the opposite direction. From the back of the base, a group of men in black combat armor immerged, two of them with missile launchers. They were accompanied by another team of advisors, covering their flanks.

"Helo's backing off. Let's move it, gentlemen!" one of them shouted.

"Alright, let's go!" another advisor shouted. Keith recognized the voice as Captain Kowal's.

They resumed digging through the rubble as quickly as possible, removing a few more bodies and dragging them to the edge of the woods behind the command post. Meanwhile, shouts and the pops of gunfire began emanating from the opposite side of the base. Once they finished moving the bodies, they regrouped around Captain Kowal.

"Dasha," Kowal looked over at the woman in the tattered business suit. "Head to the south side, Akrop and Friedman will go with you. Move as many bodies there as you can." He raised his hand to the integrated radio on his helmet, pausing for a moment. "Wilson, Jones, find your platoons and secure the west side. I'll keep you updated."

Wilson then turned to Keith. "I see you've got Marco. Where are Ambrus and Rudolph?"

"Fuck," Keith cursed aloud. "I think south-west corner." He keyed his mic, "Rudolph, Ambrus, PAR?"

Ambrus responded almost immediately. "Group 3 here! Motor pool. Burgos and Maes are dead. Earthers are all over the fuckin' place."

"Received. Rudolph, what's your status?" Another long moment passed. "Group 2, come in." Keith looked up at Wilson.

"Keith, I'm going to take Group 1 and meet up with Ambrus. Find Rudolph and report in."

Keith nodded. "You got it!"

Unslinging his rifle, Keith proceeded back to the edge of the main road, checking the horizon to his right for the helo. All clear. Just as he turned to run across the street, an armored personnel carrier stormed by nearly missing him. His shook himself.

"Today is not my day!" He took a deep breath, checked both ways, and sprinted across to the recruit tents on the opposite side. Moving as quickly as he could, he kept tripping on the veritable maze of tent stakes and cords webbing the area. Eventually making it through, he cut through a patch of trees and low growth to reach the western side of the base, a string of overgrown and dilapidated concrete buildings. Reaching them, he posted himself up at a corner.

Catching his breath, he looked up and was surprised to see a figure looking at him from the opposite corner of the building. As he regained his focus, he realized it was an Earther in full armor plate. The Earther must have been as surprised as he was, and for a split second, they just stared at each other, dumbfounded. Both then raised their rifles simultaneously, firing a few shots at each other before ducking out of sight. His back flat against the wall, Keith tried to take another deep breath, adrenalin coursing through him.

Looking to his left, he spotted a window and threw it open. Seconds later, he'd pulled himself up and in, landing with a thud on a dusty wooden floor. He flinched at the sound, though it was no louder than his heartbeat drumming in his ears. He was immediately met with the smell of moldy, stale air. Rifle up, he elected to move down a hallway to his left, gently pulling open a door and stepping in. The hallway was dark, another closed door at the end. A hole in the ceiling provided only dim illumination. When he was about halfway down it, he stopped. He swore he could hear the floor up ahead creaking.

Suddenly the sound of automatic rifle fire thundered through the building, bullets punching their way through the door up ahead and ricocheting off the walls around him. Flattening himself up against the bare concrete wall, he was lucky to have not been hit. The door itself was then kicked in half as the Earth Union soldier stormed in. Raising his rifle with one arm, Keith opened fire, striking the Earther's weapon. The Earther raised it to fire back, but there was only a click.

"Shit."

Keith attempted to reload, only to be smacked in the face by the Earther's rifle, which had been thrown across the room. The Earther then threw a haymaker, smashing Keith's weapon against the wall and forcing him to drop it. Keith tried to punch back but only succeeded in injuring his fist against the veritable wall of armor plates. The Earther answered with a left hook that Keith narrowly avoided. The punch cracked the concrete wall, raining chips down on Keith as he stumbled backward across the floor into the next room. The Earther followed, pulling a foldable shovel off his belt with one hand and flipping it open.

"Fuck you!" shouted Keith, his back against the wall.

"You first." The Earther stepped forward, raising his shovel.

Suddenly, the sound of breaking metal echoed through the room, and the Earther's head jerked right, the wall next to him sprayed with brains and blood. Keith watched as the giant collapsed to the floor, his armor rattling like some sort of broken machine. From a doorway to the right, Rudolph stepped in, rifle raised, and an odd twinkle in his eye. Once he'd examined the room for any additional threats, he looked at Keith.

"I think I've found my calling."

Keith exhaled, wanting to vomit. "Alright." He took a deep breath and started to collect himself.

Stepping over the dead Earther into the hallway, he retrieved his rifle. The handguard was split down the middle, and the sights were bent out of alignment. It'd have to do for now, though. Keith looked at the Earther's rifle on the floor. There was a bullet strike directly into its receiver, blowing it open. Not a chance that thing still worked. Keith looked back at Rudolph.

"Where are your guys?"

"Spread out over that way." Rudolph pointed a thumb over his shoulder towards the north-west corner of the base. "Fightin' Earthers right now. You're lucky I heard your shots coming in behind us."

"Yeah, yeah." Keith keyed his mic. "Advisor Wilson, Group 2 located. north-west side, over." Keith looked back at Rudolph. "Your radio work?"

"Oh," Rudolph started patting down his gear. "Think I lost it."

"I'll say it got destroyed by a bullet strike. 'Lose the radio, lose the promotion,' ya know?"

"Thanks, man! Oh, fuck." Rudolph was now peering out the doorway. "Earthers are getting close!" He brought his rifle back up to his shoulder and took position at the door's edge.

Keith keyed his mic again. "Advisor, sir, Earthers are pushing into the north-east corner!"

"Received," answered Wilson. "Have you located Group 2?"

Keith sighed, exasperated. "Yes sir. Group 2 is here!" He flinched as Rudolph opened fire.

"Hold tight. Reinforcements are coming your way."

"I... I-" Keith stumbled over the words. Looking through the doorway past Rudolph, he watched as recruit attempted to return fire against the advancing Earthers, only to get shot through the head. "Make it quick!"

Chapter 19 – Breaking Point

Keith sat in the back of the moving APC, the dim red interior lights lulling him to sleep. He'd spent the entirety of the previous day on the line fighting the Earthers. Ten hours. About halfway through the day, the Mantuans arrived, though not in the numbers expected. Combined with their firepower, UDAF was able to keep the Earthers at bay. That evening, the order came in that they were "re-positioning." To Keith, it felt like a retreat. Willing himself back awake, Keith looked down the line of seats. Only advisors in this carrier. Though it was apparent that he'd earned the respect of those around him, it was unnerving to not be among other recruits. It was like being thrown into the world of adults - as a child. Keith leaned back into his seat, stressed out.

During the withdrawal, he'd come across Gaz, who had been injured during the fighting and couldn't be moved.

"Keith, I need to do something for me," Gaz pulled a blood-stained letter from one of his pockets. "Get this to Belcher Ranch. It's important!"

Keith had argued with Gaz at the time. He'd find a way to get him aboard one of the APCs.

"Don't worry about me," he said. "The Earthers have rules for how the wounded are treated. I'll be fine!

165

Just get that letter where it needs to go." Gaz then left Keith with a warning. "Don't trust them. UDAF isn't here for us."

'Just get that letter where it needs to go.' 'Don't trust them.' The words played through Keith's head on repeat.

When Keith reached the APCs, an advisor stopped him. The advisor confiscated the letter and read it through, after which Advisor Wilson had been called over. According to them, Gaz was a spy, relying on Keith's inability to read to get the letter back to Belcher Ranch discretely. It explained Gaz's consistent interest in the advisors' activities, but Keith had a hard time believing it. At that moment, Keith pled with the advisors not to hurt Gaz. He'd heard the stories of what was done to spies in war. Much to his surprise, the advisors humored him or at least pretended to. Though reassuring at the time, Keith wasn't sure if he believed that they left Gaz alone.

"Hey," Advisor Wilson bumped Keith's shoulder. "You alright? You've got the thousand-yard stare."

"Yeah." Keith rubbed his eyes.

"It's almost your birthday, right?" asked Wilson, looking over at Keith. The red lights reflected off the lenses of his helmet, giving them an eerie glow.

"What? Yeah, yeah."

"How old you turning?"

166

"18."

"You got a girlfriend?"

Keith looked up at Wilson, equal parts annoyed and confused. "I'm not sure right now."

"Hey, whatever the case, your turning 18. We're going to celebrate. We could get you a 'temp' girlfriend if you're interested."

At this, one of the other advisors laughed. Keith eyed Wilson, confused.

"Lady of the night, if you will."

"Oh." This caught Keith off guard, leaving him anxious and excited. "Lemme think about it."

"Don't think too hard!" All the advisors laughed.

As the banter continued, Keith pulled a slip of paper out of his pocket and unfolded it. Scrawled across it was his attempt at writing. Back at Echo, Sarah always complained about Keith's illiteracy. Really that was her only complaint. He ran a finger along the chicken scratch on the page, trying to read his own handwriting. If anything, maybe the putting forth the effort would bring her back. Even with the advisor's teachings, Keith was having trouble getting a grasp of it. The letters always seemed to move around as he read them. He took a deep breath. Maybe in the morning, when the sun was out, and he could see what he was doing. He folded the paper back up and stuffed it in his pocket. For now, some sleep would do him good.

A few hours later, the APC shuttered to a stop, and Keith stepped out in a daze. A series of vivid dreams left him feeling more tired than if he'd tried to stay awake. He rubbed his eyes, then pulled the brim of his helmet a little lower.

"Hey Keith," Advisor Wilson slapped his shoulder. "You doing alright?"

"Haven't been able to sleep, sir."

Wilson looked down at Keith, his expression grim. "It happens to the best of us. Hopefully, we can get a break from this soon, get you some rest."

Keith looked up at Wilson.

Recognizing the confusion, Wilson elaborated, "The advisors here are deployed on rotation. Mine's almost up. I'm pretty sure I can convince the higher-ups to extend that to you, a little vacation."

Keith nodded.

"Also," Wilson's expression lightened up. "I've got a surprise for you. Seemed important, so I grabbed it on our way out." Wilson stepped back into the APC and retrieved

168

a leather scabbard. Keith immediately recognized it as containing his father's rifle. Wilson handed it to him. "You take care of that now. Find some shade, get some rest. We'll be setting up shop here for a bit."

"Thank you," said Keith, partially removing the lever-action from its sheath. He ran a hand along its wooden stock. It was a miracle that he still had it after all this.

Scanning the area, he picked out a large Edurucort tree and sat down underneath it. As other APCs arrived, what was left of his platoon gathered around him. Ambrus was the first to arrive, his right arm in a bloody sling. Most of his group was still with him. Marco arrived next, unscathed but shaken. His group had taken heavy casualties, and now only half remained. Rudolph arrived last, alone. He had a second rifle hanging off his back and more magazines than one could count on his vest. He seemed unphased.

Halfway through the day, as they gathered for lunch, Marco pulled Keith aside. Before he could even speak, Keith knew something was off.

"Keith," started Marco. He then paused. "This isn't for me, man. I gotta get out of here."

Keith stared at Marco, a mixture of disappointment and understanding brewing in his stomach.

"Keith, you get me?"

"Yeah." Keith sighed. "How are you going to do it?"

"I…" Marco stopped as an advisor walked by. "We're too far out to walk. I'm thinking I can grab a truck and make a run for the coast."

"You leaving is one thing, but a truck? We need those."

"I know, I know. I don't see any other way to get out of here, though. We ain't gonna win this! I don't wanna die, man!"

Keith stared at Marco. After a long pause, he spoke again. "Do what you have to. Don't let me see you."

Marco stared back at Keith, tears welling up in his eyes. "Yeah, man." He grabbed Keith's shoulder, then walked away.

"Good luck," whispered Keith.

Keith then walked silently to the newly established command center, a corrugated steel shack in the middle of this dusty field. Outside of it in the shade, he had lunch with the advisors. Fortunately for him, they took his silence as fatigue and carried on normally. As lunch ended, Keith looked over at Advisor Wilson. Noticing, Wilson looked back at Keith.

"Something on your mind?"

Keith nodded slowly. "Was Gaz really a spy? I figured that letter was for his family or something."

Wilson took a deep breath. "Yes. We'd suspected him for some time. That letter of his contained a lot of important information about us."

"Like what?"

Wilson coughed. "Tactical stuff, maps, that sorta thing."

Keith eyed Wilson, waiting for something more.

One of the other advisors then stepped up, patting Keith on the back. "He was just looking out for his people. Can't blame him for that, right?"

Wilson nodded. "Right." He then stood up and picked up the packaging leftover from his meal.

Keith looked down at his half-eaten ration pack. Best not to let anything go to waste. He began re-wrapping the food as best he could before stuffing it into his pockets. He then got up from the ground and met back up with Wilson, who was getting his gear together.

"What's the plan?"

"Well," Wilson picked up his helmet and put it on. "New Mantuan Armed Forces should be arriving early tomorrow. Depending on how things look, we'll be going on the offensive after that." Wilson picked up his rifle and slung it over his shoulder. "For now, I'd say that you can have your guys set up camp for the night. Make sure they're ready to go for the morning, though. Also, get a headcount. I'll be assigning replacements to your platoon."

"Yessir. Uhm, sir?"

"Yes?"

"A few of them are injured, what's the plan for them?"

"Unfortunately, they're going to have to ride it out. Until we push our way back west, the wounded are going to have to fight with us."

"Yes sir."

Keith walked back to the tree where he and his platoon had set up earlier. Most of the gear was still there except for a select few packs and rifles.

"Everyone, line up!" shouted Keith, his voice hoarse.

The remaining recruits got into line, Rudolph and Ambrus in front. Keith counted them silently. Thirteen recruits remaining of the original thirty, not including the group leaders.

"Yo, Keith," started Rudolph.

"What's up?" Keith asked, dryly.

"Where's Marco at?"

Keith looked down the road at a fading dust cloud. He then turned back to Rudolph. "I'm sure he's around here somewhere."

Chapter 20 - Run

It had been a busy morning thus far and the hot sun was already making its way over the treetops. Before sunrise, another group of advisors had arrived on foot, Captain Kowal and the "new man" among them. The New Mantuan Armed Forces had not made an appearance. Many of the advisors appeared anxious at best, while others were flat out pissed off. Though none had briefed Keith directly, it was obvious that something had gone wrong. Already in full kit, Keith walked to the makeshift command center.

"Your report?" asked Wilson.

"Nearly all equipment accounted for. One of the group leaders and two recruits are missing."

Wilson looked over at Keith. "Which ones?"

"Marco and two guys from his group."

Another advisor then approached Wilson. "One of our trucks is missing."

Wilson turned back to Keith. "Any idea where he would have gone?"

"Nope." Keith stared straight through Wilson, dead-eyed.

174

"Hm." Wilson nodded slightly. "We'll discuss this later. Get the platoon in order. We'll be heading out soon."

Keith nodded and turned towards the tree line where the recruits had set up their tents. All eyes were on him as he approached the remainder of his platoon. Everyone was visibly exhausted. As Keith reached them, Ambrus stepped forward.

"How you feeling, Keith?"

"Been better. Couldn't sleep." He took a deep breath. "Gather your things. We'll be heading out soon." He was about to turn back towards the command center when Ambrus stopped him.

"What was up with Marco? I saw you talking to him yesterday, then he just disappeared."

"I don't know."

Ambrus looked at Keith questioningly. When it became clear that Keith had nothing more to say, he returned to his group.

Suddenly there was an odd snapping sound, and Keith turned around just in time to see a recruit fall to the ground. As he came to realize what had happened, the pops of rifle fire began emanating from the woods in all directions.

"Get down!" Ambrus rushed forward and tackled Keith. "Fuck!" He rolled to the side and brought his rifle up as best he could with his injured arm, aiming it towards the wood line.

Many of the recruits unlucky enough to be caught standing were quickly cut down by incoming fire. The remainder began running for cover, some ducking behind the sparse few trees while others crawled up to the berms at the clearing's edges. Groups on the opposite side found themselves in the same predicament, attempting to pack men in behind limited cover that was less than a meter tall. Keith began re-orienting himself so that his front half was facing the nearest tree line. Having been caught in the open, he was hard-pressed to stay low enough to avoid enemy fire.

Keith turned to Ambrus. "Get your guys in order, I'll take care of Marco's group."

Ambrus answered with a thumbs up and began crawling towards his part of the line. Keith followed suit, breaking off to the right to meet up with what was left of Marco's guys, all two of them. Realizing the futility of coordinating a group this small, Keith directed them to follow up with Ambrus and hold tight. Peering up over the berm, he could see at least a dozen Earthers in his limited field of view. As he watched, more appeared out of the woodwork. He looked back at the recruits around him.

"Hold here, I'm going to try and get more guys!"

One of the recruits nodded, flinching as a round struck the berm above him.

"Give me some cover fire!" Staying as low as he could, Keith got up and beelined it for the command center in the middle of the field.

He made it by sheer luck, throwing open the door as a string of machinegun fire laced the wall next to him. The interior of the shack was chaos. Kowal himself and the "new man" both had rifles and were firing out of the shack's four windows. Wilson was crouched low to the floor, his left hand on the side of his helmet as he attempted to radio out. Every few seconds, a bullet would punch through one of the sheet metal walls allowing new beams of light to shine through.

"Down, Keith!" shouted Wilson, grabbing him and pulling him to the floor. "What's up?" He had to shout the words over the din.

"I've got multiple guys dead-" Keith was cut off by a nearby explosion rocking the shack. "Need reinforcements!"

"We don't have any! Other side's a mess too!" Wilson then returned his hand to the radio on the side of his helmet. "Roger that!" He looked back at Keith. "Stay here! There's no way you'll make it back there!"

Keith nodded.

Finding that his father's rifle kept bumping into walls in this tight space, he unslung it from his shoulder and put in down in a corner out of the way. Finally, he brought his issued rifle up to aim out of an unoccupied window. The trucks at the back edge of the clearing were now on fire. A nearby APC had recently been hit, and smoke was billowing out of its crew compartment. Moments later, its crew attempted to bail out, only to get gunned down as they exited. Keith fired at the Earthers coming up the road but couldn't tell if his shots met their mark. Aiming right, he tried to focus on the line where he'd left Ambrus and Rudolph. The recruits that were still alive were pinned down, barely able to return fire, or even look over the berm. An advisor managed to make it to the same berm, only to get hit as he attempted to coordinate the recruits around him. Another string of fire then struck the shack, forcing Keith back to the floor.

"Fuck!"

Keith turned to see the source of the voice. The "new man" had been struck in the belly and was now on the floor. His sunglasses were off, exposing his pained expression.

"Keep firing! I've got him!" shouted Wilson, who was already halfway to "new man."

178

Keith again stood up, deafened by the constant noise. The gunfire and explosions around him had been reduced to mere thuds in his ears. Suddenly the door next to him was thrown open, and Ambrus stumbled in, covered in dust.

"Keith!"

"What?!"

"Where those extra guys at?"

"What?" Keith moved his head closer to Ambrus, who proceeded to shout into his ear.

"Reinforcements! Are they coming?"

Keith shook his head.

Ambrus looked defeated. Having nothing more to do, he then took up a position at the window behind Keith.

"Is our evac coming?" shouted Kowal to Wilson.

"No. Earth Union forces got us on all sides. African Union's got the rest of our guys tied up!" answered Wilson.

"Shit."

As Keith reached down for another magazine, a shot grazed his helmet. Shaking himself, he turned around to see Ambrus collapse to the floor. At this, his heart started racing, and he found himself unable to breathe. He looked down at the magazine in his now shaking hand, then at his rifle. His vision was blurred, unable to focus on either. He looked back up out the window at the brightly lit clearing and the shaded tree line beyond it. He was thinking about home, his small plot back on Echo Ranch. He remembered the first Earther he killed and her pale, bloodied face. He thought about Gaz and whether he was still alive. He again looked at the rifle in his hands, the most prominent element of his promotion. It all seemed pointless.

"Farmboy, you alright?" Wilson was staring at him. "Keith? Keith!"

Keith dove out the window, ripping his helmet off as he went. As he stumbled back to his feet, the rifle was the next to go. He began his sprint across open ground, feeling the hot sun and a slight breeze on his face. Within moments he'd reached the halfway point, booking it across the clearing. He could see the tree line clearly now. He could make it.

Chapter 21 - Wasp

Sergeant Felman watched as a militiaman dove out of the shack in the middle of the clearing. Stumbling back to his feet, the young man began running for the tree line, leaving his rifle behind.

"What on Earth is he doing?" Felman said aloud.

"Two degrees west," reported Loesche.

"Got it."

Felman refocused on the target, made the appropriate adjustment, and fired. Not a moment later, the kid crumpled to the ground, unmoving.

"Good hit," reported Loesche. He then looked over at Felman. "Yeah, what was he was doing?"

Half an hour later, the conscripts had finished the job, and Felman and Loesche stepped into the clearing. First, they approached the body of the young man, flipping him over and searching through his pockets. Unlike most of the militia, his kit was new, very similar to what the mercenaries wore. Aside from a badly scrawled letter to a girlfriend, there was nothing of interest on him, though.

They then proceeded to the bullet-ridden shack in the center of the field. As Felman reached to open the door, it fell off its hinges on its own accord. He stepped in carefully, rifle raised. On the floor lay a dead militiaman and three mercenaries, back to back and riddled with bullet strikes. In a corner leaned an old-style lever action, damaged by shrapnel like everything else. Felman eyed it for a moment. It felt out of place. Regaining his focus, he stepped over the dead militiaman and went to work searching the mercenaries. The first two didn't yield anything out of the ordinary, carrying tactical maps, ammunition, and of course, communications equipment. The third had far more to offer.

Pulling off the merc's helmet, Felman was immediately struck by the man's pale complexion and bleach-white hair. Opening an eyelid and seeing a pink iris, his theory was confirmed.

"This one's a clone."

"Now that's interesting," commented Loesche, in Mars-Deutsch.

Reaching into the clone's pocket, Felman pulled out a wallet which he promptly opened. His eyes lit up as he looked over its contents.

"Got it!" exclaimed Felman, pulling out an ID card and handing it to Loesche.

182

Across the front of the card, beneath the clone's portrait were the words, "United Trade Coalition."

Loesche stared at it. "So, this was all a corporate job?"

"Looks like it." Felman turned back to the dead militiaman, flipping him over with his boot. "Do you think any of them knew?"

"Doubt it."

"Well," Felman took a deep breath. "Things are about to get real interesting."

Chapter 22 – Bykov

One Month Later - Hecate Space Station, Earth

As quickly as he could, Antonin Bykov stuffed his company apparel down the garbage disposal. First, the khaki pants, then the black collared shirts with the bronze UTC logo on the breast. Next went some of the various knick-knacks around his apartment. A gold United Trade Coalition keychain, business cards, an employee of the month award. All of it rattled its way down the disposal the same. Next, he pulled out his handgun. It was company issued, and the serial number could be traced. He stared at it for a moment. He might need it, that'd be the last to go.

He tucked the pistol into his waistband and turned toward his dresser. Throwing open the drawers, he grabbed what clothes he had left, tossing them onto the bed next to his duffel bag. Within moments the dresser was empty, and he turned towards the pile on the bed. Without the company wear, it was scant. "Yebat'!" He cursed under his breath as he began stuffing what was left of his clothes into the bag. Completely abandoning his usual sense of order, he had the bag packed and zipped up within seconds.

Hearing footsteps outside his door, he froze. Soon enough, the steps passed, and he exhaled heavily. He wiped the sweat from his brow. Best that he clean himself up real quick. He didn't need to give the guards at the terminal a reason to stop him. Stepping into the small bathroom opposite his apartment door, he splashed his face with water from the sink and tried to neaten his hair.

"Idiots! We had a nice thing going! Why did they have to get involved in politics?" Antonin muttered to himself. He stared at his reflection in the mirror. "It doesn't matter now." He grabbed a towel and dried himself. The United Trade Coalition had screwed up, and now he would be the one paying for it. Him, and hundreds of other employees stationed throughout Earth Union space. Just as was finishing up, he heard a bang on the door. He dropped the towel just in time to see a Civil Enforcement officer break it down.

They didn't say a word before they shot him.